She hoped he wouldn't come closer…

Prayed he wouldn't kiss her. "We need to forget what happened tonight," she said in a rattled voice. "We agreed it'd be crazy to—"

"Nothing really happened," he said, cutting her off.

"Well, what *almost* happened. I've made a vow to myself…and it's a promise I intend to keep. I'm never going to find what I want if I get drawn deeper into this attraction. It won't go anywhere other than your bed, and I'm not prepared to settle for just sex."

Gabe stared at her. So deeply, so intensely, she couldn't breathe. The small porch created extreme intimacy. If she took one step she'd be pressed against him.

"You're right." He moved back. "You shouldn't settle for sex. You should find that middle road you want, Lauren, with someone who can give you the quiet relationship you deserve."

Then he was gone.

Her chest was pounding. Her stomach was churning. Her head was spinning.

And her heart was in serious danger.

Dear Reader,

I'm so happy to invite you back once more to the small town of Crystal Point and to my fifth book for Harlequin Special Edition, *Once Upon A Bride*.

When Lauren Jakowski made a brief appearance in my last book I knew I wanted to give her a very special happy ending of her own. Lauren is the kind of woman I'd want to have as a friend—loyal and honest and with plenty of gumption. She's also grieving a lost love and has vowed to think with her head and not with her heart in the future. But when the supermysterious and supersexy Gabe Vitali moves in next door, she's suddenly tempted to rethink her plans. Can these two broken people find their way to one another?

I hope you enjoy *Once Upon A Bride,* and I look forward to inviting you back to Crystal Point in early 2015 for Cassie and Tanner's story.

I also love hearing from readers and can be reached via my website at www.helenlacey.com.

Warmest wishes,

Helen Lacey

Once Upon a Bride

—

Helen Lacey

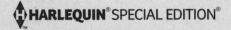

Recycling programs
for this product may
not exist in your area.

ISBN-13: 978-0-373-65839-8

ONCE UPON A BRIDE

Printed in U.S.A.

www.Harlequin.com

Books by Helen Lacey

Harlequin Special Edition

Made for Marriage #2166
Marriage Under the Mistletoe #2226
His-and-Hers Family #2238
Date with Destiny #2280
Once Upon a Bride #2357

Other books by Helen Lacey available in ebook format.

HELEN LACEY

grew up reading *Black Beauty, Anne of Green Gables* and *Little House on the Prairie*. These childhood classics inspired her to write her first book when she was seven years old, a story about a girl and her horse. She continued to write, with the dream of one day being a published author, and writing for Harlequin Special Edition is the realization of that dream. She loves creating stories about strong heroes with a soft heart and heroines who get their happily-ever-after. For more about Helen, visit her website, www.helenlacey.com.

For Robert
Because you *get* me...

Chapter One

"You made a *what?*"

Lauren Jakowski shrugged her shoulders and bit down on her lower lip, musing whether she should repeat her words. But her two best friends' imploring looks won over.

"I made a vow," she said, and glanced at both Cassie and Mary-Jayne. "Of celibacy."

The other women snorted through the drinks they were sipping, sending liquid flying across the small poolside table. It was her brother's wedding, and once the bride and groom had cut the cake and shared their first dance, her bridesmaid's duties were officially over for the night. So she'd left the hotel ballroom and met her friends by the pool.

"Yeah, sure you did," Cassie said with a laugh, wiping her face.

"I did," Lauren insisted. "When my marriage ended."

"So you, like—" Mary-Jayne mused slowly as her dark hair swayed in the breeze "—made a commitment to never have sex again?"

"Exactly," she replied. "Not until I'm certain he's the right one."

"*He* being this dull and passionless individual you think you'll find so you can have your mediocre happily ever after?" Cassie asked, watching Lauren over the rim of her glass of soda.

She ignored how absurd it sounded. "Yes."

Cassie's brows came up. "And where are you going to find this Mr. Average?" she asked. "ReliableBores.com?"

"Maybe," Lauren said, and pretended to drink some champagne.

"So no sex?" Mary-Jayne asked again. "Even though you caught the bouquet, look sensational in that dress and there are at least half a dozen single men at this wedding who would happily throw you over their shoulder, carry you off and give you the night of your life?"

"I'm not interested in anything casual," she reiterated.

Mary-Jayne's eyes widened. "Not even with—"

"Not with *anyone,*" she said firmly.

"But he's—"

The original tall, dark and handsome...

"I know what he is. And he's not on my radar."

Which was a great big lie. However, she wasn't about to admit that to her friends. Lauren stared at the flowers sitting in the center of the small table. She *had* caught the bouquet. But she didn't want some meaningless romp at her brother's wedding.

And she certainly didn't want it with Gabe Vitali.

In the past six months, she'd been within touching distance of the ridiculously good-looking American several times. *And avoided him on every single occasion.* He was exactly what she didn't want. But since he was her brother's friend—and Crystal Point was a small town—Lauren accepted that she would be forced to see him every now and then.

"I like Gabe," Mary-Jayne said, and grinned. "He's kind of mysterious and…sexy."

Lauren wrinkled her nose. "Trouble."

"But still sexy?" Cassie laughed gently. "Come on, admit it."

Lauren let out an exasperated sigh. "Okay, he's sexy. He's weak-at-the-knees sexy…. He's handsome and hot and every time I see him I wonder what he looks like out of his clothes. I said I was celibate…not comatose."

The two women laughed, and Lauren pushed aside the idea of Gabe Vitali naked.

"Still, you haven't had sex in over two years," Mary-Jayne, the more candid of the two women, reminded her. "That's a long time. Just because you got divorced doesn't mean you can't have sex."

Lauren shrugged. "Isn't there an old saying about not missing what you don't have?"

Mary-Jayne shook her head. "Please tell me you've at least *kissed* a guy since then?"

"No," she replied. "Nor do I intend to until I know he's exactly what I've been looking for."

"You mean, *planning* for," Cassie said, ever gentle. "You know, there's no neat order to falling in love."

"Who said anything about love?" Lauren pushed back her blond bangs.

Cassie's calm expression was unwavering. "Is that really what you want? A loveless relationship without passion and heat?"

Lauren shrugged. "Marriage doesn't have to be about sexual attraction. Or love."

She saw her friends' expressions, knew that even though they were both fiercely loyal and supported her unconditionally, they still thought her thinking madness. But she wasn't swayed. How could they really appreciate her feelings? Or understand what she wanted?

They couldn't.

But she knew what she wanted. No lust, no crazy chemistry. No fairy-tale love.

No risk.

"That's just grief talking," Cassie said quietly. "When a marriage breaks down, it's natural to—"

"I'm not *mourning* my divorce," she insisted. No, definitely not. Because she knew exactly what mourning felt like. "I'm glad it's over. I shouldn't have married a man I hardly knew. I've tried being in love, I've tried being in lust...and neither worked out. Believe it or not, for the first time in a long time, I actually know what I want."

"Which is?" Mary-Jayne prompted, still grinning.

Lauren smiled at her friend. "Which is an honest, uncomplicated relationship with someone I can talk to.... Someone I can laugh with...have children with...grow old with. You know, the usual things. Someone who's a friend. A companion. And not with a man who looks as though he was made to pose for an underwear ad on one of those highway billboards."

"Like Gabe?" Mary-Jayne suggested playfully, and drank some champagne. "Okay, I get it. You want short, chubby and bald...not tall, dark and handsome. But in the meantime, how about we all get back to the ballroom and find some totally *complicated* man to dance with?"

"Not me," Cassie said, and touched her four-month-pregnant belly. Her boyfriend was a soldier currently on tour in the Middle East. "But I'll happily watch from the sidelines."

Lauren shook her head. "I think I'll stay out here for a while. You two go on ahead."

Her friends took another couple of minutes to leave, and when she was alone, Lauren snatched up the colorful bouquet, stood and walked the ten feet toward the edge of the pool. Solitude crept over her skin, and she sighed. Wed-

dings always made her melancholy. Which was unfortu-
nate, since she owned the most successful bridal store in
Bellandale. Weddings were her life. Some days, though,
she thought that to be the most absurd irony.

Of course, she was pleased for her brother. Cameron
deserved every bit of happiness with his new bride, Grace
Preston. And the ceremony had been beautiful and romantic. But she had a hollow spot in her chest that ached with
a heavy kind of sadness. Many of the guests now inside
the big hotel ballroom had witnessed her union to James
Wallace in similar style three years earlier. And most knew
how it had ended. Tonight, more than ever before, Lauren's
sadness was amplified by her embarrassment at being on
the receiving end of countless pitying looks and sympa-
thetic greetings.

She took a deep breath and exhaled with a shudder.
Somehow, her dreams for the future had been lost. But
two years on, and with so many tears shed, she was stronger. And ready to start again. Only this time, Lauren would
do it right. She wouldn't rush into marriage after a three-
month whirlwind romance. And she definitely wouldn't be
swept off her feet. This time, her feet were staying firmly
on the ground.

Lauren swallowed hard, smoothed the mint-green chiffon gown over her hips and turned on her heels.

And was unexpectedly confronted with Gabe Vitali.

Stretched out on a sun lounger, tie askew and with his
black hair ruffled as if he'd been running his hand through
it, he looked so gorgeous, she literally gasped for breath. He
was extraordinarily handsome, like one of those old-time
movie stars. His glittering, blue-eyed gaze swept over her,
and a tiny smile creased the corners of his mouth.

And she knew immediately...

He'd heard.

Everything.

Every humiliating word. Heat raced up and smacked her cheeks. *Great.*

Of course, she had no logical reason to dislike him… other than the fact he was good-looking and sexy and made her insides flip-flop. But it was enough to keep her from allowing her fantasies to take over. She gripped the bouquet tighter and planted her free hand on her hip in a faux impression of control, and spoke. "Whatever you might have thought you heard, I assure you I wasn't—"

"How are the knees?" he asked as he sprang up.

He was tall, around six-two, with broad shoulders and a long-legged frame. And he looked way too good in a suit. Resentment burned through her when she realized he was referring to her earlier confession.

"Fine," she replied, dying of embarrassment inside. "Rock solid."

He came around the lounger, hands thrust into his pockets. "You're sure about that?"

Lauren glared at him. "Positive," she snapped, mortified. She wanted to flee, but quickly realized she'd have to squeeze herself in between him and the sun lounger if she wanted to make a getaway. "I think I'll return to the ballroom now, if you don't mind."

His mouth curled at the edges. "You know, just because someone knows your vulnerabilities, it doesn't necessarily make him your enemy."

Lauren's skin heated. *"Vulnerabilities?"* She sucked in a sharp breath. "I don't quite know what you mean by that, but if you're insinuating that I'm *vulnerable* because I haven't… Because I… Well, because it's been a while since I was…you know…" Her words trailed off as mortification clung to every pore. Then she got annoyed as a quick cover-up. "Let's get this straight. I'm not the least bit vulnerable. Not to you or to anyone *like* you."

He grinned. "Whoa. Are you always so prickly?"

Prickly? She wasn't *prickly.* She was even tempered and friendly and downright *nice.*

She glared at him. "Do you always eavesdrop on private conversations?"

"I was simply relaxing on a pool lounger," he replied smoothly, his accent so delicious, it wound up her spine like liquid silk. "And I was here before you, remember? The fact you spoke about your sex life so openly is really no one's fault but your own." One brow rose. "And although it was entertaining, there's no need to take your frustration out on—"

"I am not *frustrated,*" she snapped, figuring he was probably referring to her being sexually starved in some misguided, macho way. Broad shoulders, blue eyes and nice voice aside, he was a jerk. "I just don't want to talk about it anymore. What I'd like is to forget this conversation ever happened."

"I'm sure you would."

Lauren wanted a big hole to open up and suck her in. When one didn't appear, she took a deep breath. "So we have a deal. I'll ignore you, and you can ignore me. That way we never have to speak to each other again."

"Since this is the first time we have actually spoken," he said, his gaze deep enough to get lost in. "I don't think it will be a hardship."

He was right. They'd never spoken. She'd made sure of it. Whenever he was close, she'd always managed to make a quick getaway. Lauren sniffed her dislike, determined to ignore the fact that the most gorgeous man she'd ever met probably thought she was stark raving mad. And she would have done exactly that. Except she turned her heel too quickly, got caught between the tiles, and seconds later, she was tumbling in a cartwheel of arms and legs and landed into the pool, bouquet flying, humiliation complete.

The shock of hitting the water was quickly interrupted

when a pair of strong hands grasped one arm, then another. In seconds, she was lifted up and over the edge of the pool and set right on her feet.

He still held her, and had his hands intimately positioned on her shoulders.

She should have been cold through to her bones. But she wasn't. She was hot. All over. Her saturated dress clung to every dip and curve, her once carefully styled hair was now draping down her neck and her blood burned through her veins like a grass fire.

"Steady," he said softly, holding her so close she could see the tiny pulse in his jaw.

Lauren tried to speak, tried to move, tried to do something, *anything,* other than shake in his arms and stare up into his handsome face. But she failed. Spectacularly. It was he who eventually stepped back. When he finally released her, Lauren's knees wobbled and she sucked in a long breath to regain her composure. Of which she suddenly had none. He looked at her, *over her,* slowly and provocatively and with just enough male admiration to make her cheeks flame. She glanced down and shuddered. The sheer, wet fabric hugged her body like a second skin and left *nothing* to the imagination.

She moved her lips. "I should…I think I should…"

"Yes," he said quietly when her words trailed. "You probably should."

Lauren shifted her feet and managed one step backward, then another. Water dripped down her arms and legs, and she glanced around for a towel or something else to cover herself. When she couldn't find anything suitable, she looked back at him and noticed he still watched her. Something passed between them, a kind of heady, intense awareness that rang off warning bells in her head and should have galvanized her wobbly knees into action. But she couldn't move.

Seconds later, he shrugged out of his jacket and quickly draped it around her shoulders. The warmth from the coat and his nearness enveloped her like a protective cloak, and Lauren expelled a long sigh. She didn't want to feel that. Didn't want to *think* that. She only wanted to escape.

"Thank you," she whispered. "I appreciate—"

"Forget it," he said, cutting her off. "You should get out of those wet clothes before you catch a cold," he said, and then stepped back.

Lauren nodded, turned carefully and rushed from the pool area, water and humiliation snapping at her heels.

One week later Gabe pulled the for-sale peg from the ground, stuck the sign in the crook of his arm and headed across the front yard. The low-set, open-plan brick-and-tile home was big and required a much-needed renovation. But he'd bought the house for a reasonable price, and it seemed as good a place as any to settle down.

And he was happy in Crystal Point. The oceanfront town was small and friendly, and the beaches and surf reminded him of home. He missed California, but he enjoyed the peacefulness of the small Australian town he now called home instead. He'd rented a place in the nearby city of Bellandale for the past few months, but he liked the seaside town much better. Bellandale, with its sixty thousand residents, was not as populated as Huntington Beach, Orange County, where he'd lived most of his life. But it was busy enough to make him crave the solitude and quiet of Crystal Point. Plus, he was close to the beach and his new job.

He liked the job, too. Managing the Crystal Point Surf Club & Community Center kept him occupied, and on the weekends, he volunteered as a lifeguard. The beach was busy and well maintained, and so far he'd only had to administer first aid for dehydration and a couple of jellyfish stings. Nothing life threatening. Nothing he couldn't handle. Nothing that made him dwell on all he'd given up.

Gabe fished the keys from his pocket, dropped the sign into the overgrown garden bed and climbed the four steps to the porch. His household items had arrived that morning, and he'd spent most of the day emptying boxes and wishing he'd culled more crap when he'd put the stuff into storage six months ago. His cousin, Scott, had offered to come and give him a hand unpacking, but Gabe wasn't in the mood for a lecture about his career, his personal life or anything else.

All his energy would go into his job and renovating the house, which he figured would keep him busy for six months, at least. After that, he'd tackle the yard, get the place in shape and put the house on the market again. How hard could it be? His brother Aaron did the same thing regularly. True, he wasn't much of a carpenter, and Aaron was a successful builder in Los Angeles, but he'd give it a shot.

He headed inside and flicked on some lights. Some of the walls were painted black, no doubt a legacy from the previous tenants—a group of twenty-something heavy-metal enthusiasts who were evicted for cultivating some suspicious indoor plants—so painting was one of the first things on the agenda. The kitchen was neat and the bathrooms bearable. And although the furniture he'd bought a few months ago looked a little out of place in the shabby rooms, once the walls and floors were done, he was confident it would all look okay.

Gabe tossed the keys in a bowl on the kitchen table and pulled his cell from his pocket. He noticed there were a couple of missed calls. One from Aaron and another from his mother. It would be around midnight in California, and he made a mental note to call them back in the morning. Most days he was glad the time difference let him off the hook when it came to dealing with his family. At least his

younger brother, Luca, and baby sister, Bianca, didn't stick
their nose into his life or moan about his decision to move
to Crystal Point. As the eldest, Aaron always thought he
knew best, and his mom was just…Mom. He knew she
worried, knew his mom and Aaron were waiting for him
to relapse and go running back to California.

He'd come to Crystal Point to start over, and the house
and job were a part of that new life. Gabe liked that his family wasn't constantly around to dish out advice. Bad enough
he got lectures on tap from Scott. Hell, he understood their
motives…he might even have done the same thing had
the situation been reversed. But things had changed. *He'd*
changed. And Gabe was determined to live his life, even
if it wasn't the one he'd planned on.

The private cul-de-sac in Crystal Point was an ideal
place to start. It was peaceful, quiet and uncomplicated.
Just what he wanted. A native bird squawked from somewhere overhead and he stared out the kitchen window and
across the hedge to the next house along just as his cell
rang. He looked at the screen. It was an overseas number
and not one he recognized.

Uncomplicated?

Gabe glanced briefly out the window again as he answered the call. It was Cameron Jakowski, and the conversation lasted a couple of minutes. *Sure, uncomplicated.*
Except for his beautiful, blonde, brown-eyed neighbor.

The thing about being a *go-to,* agreeable kind of
person…sometimes it turned around to bite you on the
behind. And this, Lauren thought as she drove up the driveway and then pulled up under the carport, was probably
going to turn out to be one of those occasions.

Of course, she *could* have refused. But that wasn't really her style. She knew her brother wouldn't have called if

there was any other option. He'd asked for her help, and she would always rally her resolve when it came to her family.

What she didn't want to do—what she was *determined* to avoid doing—was start up any kind of conversation with her new next-door neighbor. Bad enough he'd bought the house and moved in just days after the never-to-be-spoken-about and humiliating event at the wedding. The last thing she wanted to do was knock on his door.

Ever.

Lauren had hoped to never see him again. But it seemed fate had other ideas.

She took a breath, grabbed her bag and jacket and stepped out of the car. She struggled to open the timber gate that she'd been meaning to get repaired for the past three months and winced when the jagged edge caught her palm. Once inside her house, she dumped her handbag and laptop in the hall and took a few well-needed breaths.

I don't want to do this....

But she'd promised Cameron.

And a promise is a promise....

Then she headed next door.

Once she'd rounded the tall hedge, Lauren walked up the gravel path toward the house. There was a brand-new Jeep Cherokee parked in the driveway. The small porch illuminated with a sensor light once she took the three steps. The light flickered and then faded. She tapped on the door and waited. She heard footsteps before the door swung back on its hinges, and she came face-to-face with him.

And then butterflies bombarded her stomach in spectacular fashion.

Faded jeans fitted lean hips, and the white T-shirt he wore accentuated a solid wall of bronzed and very fine-looking muscle. His short black hair, clean-shaven jaw and body to die for added up to a purely lethal combination.

He really is gorgeous.

Memories of what had happened by the pool came rushing back. His hands on her skin, his glittering gaze moving over her, his chest so close she could almost hear his heartbeat. Mesmerized, Lauren sucked in a breath. He knew all about her. He knew things she'd told only her closest friends. He knew she'd thought about him…and imagined things.

But if he dares say anything about my knees being weak, I'll…

She finally found her voice. "I'm here…"

One brow cocked. "So I see."

"Did Cameron—"

"He called," he said, and smiled as he interrupted her.

"Is he…"

"He is." He jerked his thumb over his shoulder and toward the door behind him. "Safe and sound and flaked out in front of the television."

She ignored the smile that tried to make its way to her lips and nodded. "Okay, thank you."

When she didn't move, he looked her over. "Are you coming inside or do you plan on camping on my doorstep all night?"

"All night?" she echoed, mortified that color was creeping up her neck. The idea of doing *anything* all night with Gabe Vitali took the temperature of her skin, her blood and pretty much every other part of her anatomy up a few notches. "Of course not."

He dropped his arms to his sides and stepped back.

Lauren crossed the threshold and walked into the hall. He was close, and everything about him affected her on a kind of sensory level. As much as she didn't want to admit anything, she was attracted to him. And worse luck, he knew it.

Her vow of celibacy suddenly seemed to be dissolving into thin air.

She walked down the short hallway and into the huge, open-plan living area. The furniture looked new and somehow out of place in the room. And sure enough, on the rug in front of the sofa, was her brother's one hundred and fifty pound French Mastiff, Jed. Fast asleep and snoring loudly.

"Thanks for picking him up from my brother's place," she said as politely as she could. "When Cameron called this morning, he said the house sitter had left quickly."

He nodded. "Her daughter is having a baby. She took a flight out from Bellandale after lunch and said she'd be back in a week."

Lauren bit down on her lip. "A week?"

"That's what she said."

A week of dog-sitting. Great. As much as she liked Jed, he was big, needy, had awful juicy jowls and a reputation for not obeying anyone other than Cameron. Too bad her parents had a cat that ruled the roost, or she would have dropped him off there. She had to admit the dog seemed comfortable draped across Gabe's rug.

She looked around some more. "So…you've moved in?"

"That was the general idea when I bought the house," he replied.

Lauren's teeth ground together. "Of course. I hope you'll be very happy here."

She watched his mouth twist with a grin. "You do? Really?"

"Really," she said, and raised a disinterested brow. "Be happy, or don't be happy. It's nothing to do with me."

His blue eyes looked her up and down with way too much leisure. The mood quickly shifted on a whisper of awareness that fluttered through the air and filled up the space between them. A change that was impossible to ignore, and there was rapidly enough heat in the room to combust a fire.

Warmth spread up her neck. He had a way of doing that to her. A way of heating her skin. "I need to…I need…"

"I think we both know what you need."

Sex…

That was what he was thinking. Suddenly, that was what *she* was thinking, even though turning up on his doorstep had nothing to do with her *lacking* love life or her vow to stay celibate. Lauren's cheeks burned, and her knees trembled. "I don't know what—"

"You don't like me much, do you?" he asked, cutting her off with such calm self-assurance, she wanted to slug him.

"I'm not—"

"Or is it because you *do* like me much?" he asked, cutting her off yet again. "And that's why you're so rattled at being in my living room."

Conceited jerk! Lauren sucked in some air, pushed back her shoulders and called Jed to heel. By the time the dog got up and ambled toward her, she was so worked up she could have screamed. She grasped Jed's collar and painted on a smile. "Thank you for collecting him from Cameron's."

"My pleasure."

Pleasure? Right. Not a word she wanted to hear from him. Not a word she wanted to think about in regard to him. And when she was safely back in her own home, Lauren kept reminding herself of one thing…Mr. Right was *not* Mr. Right-Next-Door.

Chapter Two

It was the dress.

That was why he'd had Lauren Jakowski on his mind for the past week.

When Gabe pulled her from the pool, the wet fabric had stuck to her curves so erotically, it had taken his breath away. She was as pretty as hell. A couple of years back he wouldn't have hesitated in coming on to her. He would have lingered by the pool, made small talk, flirted a little, asked her out and gotten her between the sheets by the third date. But he wasn't that man anymore.

Not so long ago, there had been no short supply of women in his life and in his bed. He'd mostly managed to keep things casual until he met Mona. She was the daughter of a colleague, and after dating for six months, they'd moved in together. At thirty years of age, he'd convinced himself it was time he got around to settling down. Gabe had a girlfriend, a career he loved, a nice apartment and good friends. Life was sweet. Until everything had blown up in his face.

Eighteen months later, he was in Crystal Point, working at the surf club and trying to live a normal life. A life that didn't include a woman like Lauren Jakowski.

Because she was too...wholesome.

Too...perfect.

A beautiful blonde with caramel eyes and porcelain skin. *Exactly my type.*

But by the pool, she'd made it clear to her friends what she was looking for—stability, reliability, longevity. And since he couldn't offer her any of those things, she was everything he needed to avoid. He didn't want her turning up on his doorstep. He didn't want to inhale the scent of the flowery fragrance that clung to her skin. And he certainly didn't want to remember how it felt to have her lovely curves pressed against him.

The best thing would be to ignore her...just as she'd suggested.

Damned inconvenient, then, that he'd bought the house right next door. If he'd known that before he'd signed on the dotted line, he might have changed his mind. But it was too late to think about that now. All he had to do was get through the renovation and the resale without remembering that she was merely over the hedge.

Lauren was not one-night-stand material...and he couldn't offer anything more.

Gabe dropped into the sofa and flicked channels on the television for half an hour before he thought about eating something. He headed to the kitchen and stopped in his tracks when he spotted the pile of canine accessories by the back door. Damn. He'd forgotten about that. When Cameron had called and asked him to make an emergency stop at his home to collect the dog, the vacating house sitter had thrust the bed, bowls, food and lead into his arms along with a note listing feeding instructions. Things that Lauren would need.

Realizing there was little point in avoiding the inevitable, Gabe shoved his feet into sneakers, swung the bag of dog food over one shoulder, grabbed the rest of the gear and his house keys and headed next door.

Lauren's home and gardens were neat and tidy, and the only thing that seemed out of place was the rickety gate. He pushed it open and headed up the steps. The porch light was on and the front door open, so he tapped on the security screen. From somewhere in the house, he could hear her talking to the dog, and the obvious frustration in her voice made him smile. Maybe she was more a cat person? He tapped again and then waited until he heard her footsteps coming down the hall.

"Oh…hi," she said breathlessly when she reached the door.

Her hair was mussed and her shirt was pulled out from the front of her skirt, and Gabe bit back a grin. She looked as if she'd been crash tackled on the thirty-yard line. "Everything all right?"

She glanced over her shoulder. "Fine."

Gabe didn't quite believe her. "I forgot to give you this."

Her mouth set in a serious line. "Just leave it out there and I'll grab it later."

"It's heavy," he said, and jangled the bag of kibble resting on his shoulder. "I should probably set it down inside."

She looked at him for a second and then unlocked the screen. "Okay. Take it to the kitchen, at the end of the hall."

Gabe pushed the screen back and crossed the threshold. When he passed the living room doorway he immediately figured out the reason for her distress. Stretched out with legs in the air and jowls drooping, the dog was rolling around on her flowery chintz sofa.

"Jed looks as though he's made himself comfortable," he said, and kept walking.

"Yes, very comfortable."

When they reached the kitchen, Gabe swiveled on his heels and stared at her. She had her arms folded, her chin up and her lips pressed together, and even though she looked like she'd rather eat arsenic than spend a moment in his company, Gabe couldn't stop thinking about how beautiful she was.

I haven't gotten laid in a while...that's all it is.

He wasn't conceited, but he'd heard enough by the pool that night to know the attraction was mutual. He also knew she clearly thought it was as impossible as he did. Which suited him just fine. He didn't want to be stirred by her. He didn't want to spend restless nights thinking about having her in his bed.

"Where do you want it?" he asked.

"By the door will do."

He placed the gear on the floor and turned around to face her. "Would you like me to remove him from your sofa?"

"How did you know I couldn't...?"

"He's got about thirty pounds on you," Gabe said when her words trailed. "I just figured."

She shrugged. "I tried dragging him off, but he's as heavy as lead."

Gabe smiled and withdrew the note from his pocket. "Feeding instructions," he said, and dropped the paper onto the countertop. "If you want to get his food sorted, I'll get him off the sofa."

"Thank you," she said, then laid her hands on the back of a dining chair and grimaced. "Ouch."

He saw her shake her hand. "What's wrong?"

"Nothing," she replied and shook her hand again. "Just a splinter I got earlier from my gate."

"Let me see."

She curled her hand. "It's nothing."

Gabe moved around the kitchen counter. "It might become infected," he said, suddenly serious. "Do you have a first-aid kit?"

"It's nothing, really."

"It won't take a minute," he insisted. "So your first-aid kit?"

She shook her head. "I don't like needles."

"Don't be a baby."

Her eyes flashed, and she pushed her shoulders back as she marched into the kitchen and opened the pantry. "Here," she said, and tossed something through the air.

Gabe caught it one-handed and placed the kit on the table. "I'll be gentle. Sit," he said, and pulled out a chair.

She glared again, and he marveled that she still managed to look stunning with a scowl on her face. She sat down and waited while he dropped into a chair opposite.

"Hand?"

She pushed her hand into the center of the table and turned it over. "Gentle, remember?"

He smiled, opened the kit and took out an alcohol swab and an individually wrapped needle. When he took hold of her fingertips, his entire body crackled with a kind of heady electricity. Being so close wasn't helping his determination to steer clear of her.

"So what kind of work do you do?" he asked to try to get his mind off her soft skin and flowery perfume.

"I own a bridal shop in Bellandale."

He stretched out her palm. "That sounds interesting."

"Does it?"

Gabe looked up. She really did have the most amazing brown eyes. Warm and deep and intoxicating. She was remarkably beautiful, and he doubted she even knew it.

"Just making conversation," he said.

Her brows shot up. "To what end?"

"Are you always so suspicious?" he asked.

"Of what?"

"People," he replied. "Men."

She tensed, and Gabe held her hand a little firmer. "Not usually," she said quietly.

So it was just him? "I don't have any sinister intentions. So relax," he said as he extracted the splinter without her noticing at first and then gently rolled her fingers into her palm. "I'm not making a pass."

She swallowed hard. "I didn't think—"

"I would," he said quietly. "If you were looking for a no-strings, no-commitment kind of thing. But you're not. You're a commitment kind of girl, right? Abstaining from anything casual and with a clear plan for your future. Isn't that why you made your vow of celibacy?"

It felt right to get it out in the open. Maybe it would help diffuse the heat between them. Maybe it would stop him from thinking about kissing her.

She jerked her hand back and stood. "I... What I said at the wedding... It was private and personal and not up for discussion."

"I'm not mocking you," he said, and rested his elbows on the table. "On the contrary, I think I admire you for knowing what you want. And knowing what you don't."

Lauren's skin burned. He admired her? He'd pretty much admitted he wanted her, too. The awareness between them intensified, and she wished she could deny it. She wanted to dislike him. She wanted to resent him. She wanted to get away and never speak to him again.

"Thank you for the first aid," she said, and managed a tight smile. "I didn't feel a thing."

"Then we should keep it that way."

There was no mistaking his meaning. He thought it was a bad idea, too. She was happy about that. Very happy.

"So…about the dog?"

He stood up and pushed the chair back. "Get his feed ready and I'll drag him off your sofa."

Once he'd left the kitchen and disappeared down the hall, Lauren got to her feet and quickly sorted the dog's bedding and food in the laundry. A couple of minutes later, Gabe returned with Jed at his side. The dog ambled across the kitchen and into the back room and began eating.

Relieved the hound was no longer taking up her couch, Lauren took a shallow breath. "Thank you…Gabe."

He looked a little amused by her sudden use of his name and the slight tremor in her voice. His mouth twisted fractionally, as if he was trying not to smile. "No problem… Lauren."

"Well…good night."

His glittering gaze was unwavering. "I'll see you tomorrow."

Her eyes widened. "Tomorrow?"

He grinned a little. "I told Cameron I'd take the dog to work tomorrow so he doesn't destroy your yard trying to escape…until you can make other arrangements, of course."

She hadn't spared a thought to how she would care for the dog during the day. "Oh, right," she said vaguely, thinking about how the darn dog had suddenly become a reason why she would be forced to interact with Gabe. She made a mental note to call her friend Mary-Jayne and ask her to help. Lauren knew one thing—she didn't want to turn up on Gabe's doorstep again. "I'll tie him in the back when I leave, and you can collect him from there. You don't start until ten tomorrow, right?"

Gabe frowned. "How do you know that?"

"Cameron left me the roster," she replied. "I said I'd work the Sunday shifts while he's away if I'm needed."

"You're the fill-in lifeguard?"

"Don't look so surprised."

"I'm just curious as to why your brother didn't mention you specifically."

She shrugged a little. "I may have told him that I thought you were an ass."

Gabe laughed. "Oh, really?"

"It was after the wedding, so who could blame me?"

He raised his hands. "Because I innocently overheard your deepest secret?"

"Well, that was before I…" Her words trailed. Before what? Before she realized he wasn't quite the ogre she'd pegged him for. Now wasn't the time to admit anything. "Anyhow…good night."

Once he left, Lauren forced herself to relax. She took a long shower and changed into her silliest short-legged giraffe pajamas and made a toasted cheese sandwich for dinner. She ate in the lounge room, watching television, legs crossed lotus-style, with plans to forget all about her neighbor.

And failed.

Because Gabe Vitali reminded her that she was a flesh-and-blood woman in every sense of the word. The way he looked, the way he walked with that kind of natural sexual confidence, the way his blue eyes glittered… It was all too easy to get swept away thinking about such things.

And too easy to forget why she'd vowed to avoid a man like him at all costs.

She'd made her decision to find someone steady and honest and ordinary. No powerful attraction. No blinding lust. No foolish dreams of romantic love. Just friendship and compatibility. It might sound boring and absurd to her friends, but Lauren knew what she wanted. She wanted something lasting.

Something safe.

Since she spent most of the night staring at the ceiling, Lauren wasn't surprised when she awoke later than usual and had to rush to get ready for work. She fed the dog and then tied him on a generous lead to the post on her back patio and headed to the store. Her mother was there already, changing mannequins and merchandising the stock that had arrived Friday afternoon. Irene Jakowski had first opened The Wedding House twenty-five years earlier. Lauren had grown up around the gowns and the brides, and it had made her fall in love with weddings. During her school years, she'd worked part-time in the store, learning from her mother. When school finished, she'd studied business and accounting for two years at college before returning to the store, taking over from her mother, who now worked part-time.

Lauren dropped her laptop and bag on the desk in the staff room and headed to the sales floor. The rows of wedding gowns, each one immaculately pressed and presented on hangers, filled her with a mix of approval and melancholy.

"How's the dog?" her mother queried when she moved around the sales counter.

Lauren grimaced. "Missing his owner and slobbering all over my furniture. You know, like in that old movie *Turner & Hooch?*"

Irene laughed. "It's not that bad, surely?"

"Time will tell," she replied, and managed a rueful grin. "I don't know why he can't go into a boarding kennel like other dogs."

"You're brother says he pines when he's away from home," Irene told her. "And it's only until the house sitter returns, isn't it?"

"Yeah," Lauren said, and sighed. "Gabe is taking him to the surf club today, so at least my patio furniture is safe while I'm here."

Her mother's eyes widened. "Gabe is? Really?"

Of course her mother knew Gabe Vitali. She'd mentioned him several times over the past six months. Irene Jakowski was always on the lookout for a new son-in-law, since the old one hadn't worked out. The fact he'd bought the house next door was like gold to a matchmaking parent.

"Matka," Lauren warned, using the Polish word for *mother* when she saw the familiar gleam in her mother's eyes. "Stop."

"I was only—"

"I know what you're doing," Lauren said, smiling. "Now, let's get the store open."

By the time Gabe returned home that afternoon, he was short on patience and more than happy to hand Jed over to his neighbor. Damned dog had chewed his car keys, his sneakers and escaped twice through the automatic doors at the clubhouse.

When he pulled into the driveway, he spotted the fencing contractor he'd called earlier that day parked across the lawn. He locked Jed in Lauren's front garden and headed back to his own yard. He was twenty minutes into his meeting with the contractor when she arrived home. Gabe was in the front yard with the tradesman, talking prices and time frames, as the older man began pushing at the low timber fence that separated the two allotments and then wrote in a notepad.

She walked around the hedge and met him by the letterbox, eyeing the contractor's battered truck suspiciously. "What's going on?" she asked, looking all business in her black skirt and white blouse.

"A new fence," Gabe supplied and watched her curiosity quickly turn into a frown.

"I wasn't aware *we* needed a new one."

"This one's falling down," he said, and introduced her to the contractor before the other man waved his notepad and said he'd get back to him tomorrow.

Once the battered truck was reversing from the yard, she clamped her hands to her hips. "Shouldn't we have discussed it first?"

"It's only an estimate," he told her. "Nothing's decided yet."

She didn't look convinced. "Really?"

"Really," he assured her. "Although the fence does need replacing."

Her eyes flashed. "I know it's my responsibility to pay for half of any fence that's built, but at the moment I'm—"

Gabe shook his head. "I intend to pay for the fence, should it come to that."

She glared at him, then the fence, then back to him. "You don't get to decide that for me," she snapped, still glaring.

He looked at her, bemused by her sudden annoyance. "I don't?"

"It's my fence, too."

"Of course," he replied. "I was only—"

"Taking over? And probably thinking I couldn't possibly afford it and then feeling sorry for me, right?"

He had a whole lot of feelings churning through his blood when it came to Lauren Jakowski...pity definitely wasn't one of them. "Just being neighborly," he said, and figured he shouldn't smile, even though he wanted to. "But hey, if you want to pay for half the fence, go ahead."

"I will," she replied through tight lips. "Just let me know how much and when."

"Of course," he said.

She huffed a little. "Good. And have you been messing around with my gate?"

Ah. So the real reason why she looked like she wanted to slug him. "Yes, I fixed your gate this morning."

"Because?"

"Because it was broken," he replied, watching her temper flare as the seconds ticked by. *And broken things should be fixed.* He'd spent most of his adult life fixing things. *Fixing people.* But she didn't know that. And he wasn't about to tell her. "No point risking more splinters."

"I liked my gate how it was," she said, hands still on hips.

Gabe raised a brow. "Really?"

She scowled. "Really."

"You're mad at me because I repaired your gate?"

"I'm mad at you because it wasn't your gate to repair. I don't need anyone to fix things. I don't need a white knight, okay?"

A white knight? Yeah, right. But there was an edge of vulnerability in her voice that stopped him from smiling. Was she broken? Was that part of what drew him to her? Like meets like? He knew she was divorced, and at her brother's wedding she'd admitted her marriage hadn't been a happy one. But Gabe didn't want to speculate. And he didn't want to ask. The less he knew, the better.

"Okay," he said simply.

For a moment, he thought she might argue some more. Instead, she dropped her gaze and asked an obvious question. "What happened to your shoe?"

He glanced down. The back of his left sneaker was torn and the lace was missing. "Jed."

She looked up again, and he saw her mouth curve. "Was that the only damage?"

"Other than chewing my car keys and making a run for it whenever he got the chance."

She moaned softly. "Sorry about that. I'll get Cameron to replace them when he gets back."

Gabe shrugged. "No need. It's only a shoe."

She nodded, turned and walked back around the hedge. Gabe shook his shoulders and made a concerted effort to forget all about her.

And failed.

I really need to stop reacting like that.

Lauren was still thinking it forty minutes later when she emerged from the shower and pulled on frayed gray sweats. Her reaction, or rather her *overreaction,* to Gabe's news about the fence was amplified by his interference with her gate.

She didn't want him fixing things.

Lauren didn't want *any* man fixing things.

It was a road she'd traveled before. She knew what she wanted and white knights need not apply. Her ex-husband had tried to fix things—to fix her—and it had ended in disaster.

James Wallace had ridden into her life in his carpenter's truck, all charm and good looks. He'd arrived at The Wedding House to make repairs to the changing rooms, and she'd been unexpectedly drawn to his blatant flirting. An hour later, she'd accepted his invitation to go out with him that night. They ended up at a local bistro for drinks and then dinner, and by midnight he'd kissed her in the car park, and she was halfway in lust with him.

Three months later, she had a fairy-tale wedding.

Even though it was the wedding she'd planned to have to someone else.

To Tim. Sweet, handsome Tim Mannering. Her first love. Her only love. He had been her college boyfriend and the man she'd intended to marry. They'd made plans for the future. They'd talked about everything from building their dream home, taking an African-safari vacation, to how many kids they would have. They'd loved one another deeply and promised each other the world.

Except Tim had died three weeks before their wedding.

And Lauren walked down the aisle with another man less than two years later.

She swallowed the tightness in her throat. Thinking about Tim still filled her with sadness. And she was sad about James, too. She should never have married him. She hadn't loved him. They'd shared a fleeting attraction that had faded just months into their marriage. They'd had little in common and very different dreams. Within a year, James was gone, tired of what he called her *cold, unfeeling heart.* And Lauren was alone once more.

But she still hoped to share her life with someone. And she wanted the children she'd planned for since the day she and Tim had become engaged. Only next time, Lauren was determined to go into it with her eyes wide-open and not glazed over by romantic illusions. What she'd had with James wasn't enough. And what she'd had with Tim had left her broken inside. Now all she wanted was the middle road. Just mutual respect, trust and compatibility. No fireworks. No deep feelings. Lust was unreliable. Love was painful when lost.

There was nothing wrong with settling. Nothing at all. Settling was safe. All she had to do was remember what she wanted and why. And forget all about Gabe Vitali and his glittering blue eyes and broad shoulders. Because he was pure heartbreak material. And her heart wasn't up for grabs.

Not now.

Not ever again.

Chapter Three

Gabe went to his cousin's for dinner Wednesday night and expected the usual lecture about his life. Scott Jones was family and his closest friend, and even though he knew the other man's intentions were born from a sincere interest in his well-being, Gabe generally pulled no punches when it came to telling his cousin to mind his own business.

Scott's wife, Evie, was pure earth mother. She was strikingly attractive and possessed a calm, generous spirit. Gabe knew his cousin was besotted with his wife and baby daughter, and he was genuinely happy for him.

"How's the house coming along?" Scott asked over a beer while Evie was upstairs putting little Rebecca down for the night.

Gabe pushed back in the kitchen chair. "Fine."

"Will you stay there permanently?"

"I doubt it," he replied.

"Still can't see you renovating the place yourself," Scott said, and grinned.

Gabe frowned. "I can fix things."

Like Lauren's gate, which hadn't gone down so well. He should have left it alone. But she'd hurt herself on the thing and he didn't want that happening again. There was no harm in being neighborly.

"Job still working out?"

Gabe shrugged one shoulder. "Sure."

Scott grinned again. "And how's it going with your next-door neighbor?"

He knew his cousin was fishing. He'd told him a little about the incident at the wedding, and Scott knew he'd bought the house next door. Clearly, he'd told him too much. "Fine."

"I like Lauren," Scott said, and smiled.

Gabe didn't respond. He didn't have to. His cousin spoke again.

"You do, too, judging by the look on your face."

Gabe didn't flinch. "You know my plans. They haven't changed."

"Your five-year plan?" Scott's eyes widened. "Still think you can arrange life to order?" He looked to the ceiling, clearly thinking about his family upstairs. "No chance."

"I know what I'm doing."

It sounded good, at least. Pity he didn't quite believe it.

"You know she's divorced?" Scott asked.

"Yes."

Scott nodded. "Evie knows more about it than I do. And, of course, about the other guy."

His head came up. The other guy? "I don't—"

"He died about five years ago," his cousin said, and drank some beer. "They were engaged, that's all I know."

Gabe's insides contracted. So she'd lost someone. And married someone else. The wrong someone else. It explained the haunted, vulnerable look shading her brown eyes. But he didn't want to know any more. Hadn't he already decided the less he knew, the better?

"Not my business."

Scott's eyebrows shot up. "So no interest at all?"

He shrugged again. "No."

Scott chuckled. "You're a lousy liar."

I'm a great liar. His whole life was a lie. Gabe stood and scraped the chair back. "Thanks for the beer."

He left shortly after, and by the time he pulled into his own driveway, it was past ten o'clock. There were lights on next door, and when he spotted a shadowy silhouette pass by the front window, Gabe fought the way his stomach churned thinking about her. He didn't want to be thinking, imagining or anything else. Lauren Jakowski was a distraction he didn't need.

And he certainly didn't expect to find her on his doorstep at seven the next morning.

But there she was. All perfection and professionalism in her silky blue shirt and knee-length black skirt. Once he got that image clear in his head, Gabe noticed she wasn't alone. Jed sat on his haunches at her side.

"Am I stretching the boundaries of friendship?" she asked, and held out the lead.

He nodded. Were they friends now? No. Definitely not. "Absolutely."

She chewed at her bottom lip. "I wouldn't ask if it wasn't important."

Gabe shrugged. "What's the big emergency?"

She exhaled heavily. "He chewed off a piece of my sofa and broke the table in the living room when I left him home on Tuesday. Then he terrorized my parents' cat when I left him there yesterday. Mary-Jayne said she'd take him tomorrow and Saturday. She's got a fully enclosed yard and a dog, which will keep him company. But today I'm all out of options. I can't take him to the store and...and...I don't know what else to do."

Her frustration was clear, and Gabe knew he'd give her exactly what she wanted. Because saying no to Lauren was becoming increasingly difficult. "Okay."

"O-okay?" she echoed hesitantly.

"Yeah. Okay."

Relief flooded her face. "Thanks. I...I owe you for this."

Gabe shrugged again. He didn't want her owing him anything. Owing could lead to collecting...and that was out of the question. "No problem," he said, and took the lead.

"So dinner?" she asked and took a step back. "Tonight. I'll cook. My way of saying thanks."

His back straightened. "You don't need to—"

"I insist," she said quickly, and then looked as though she was itching to get away. "Say, seven o'clock?"

She left, and Gabe didn't go back inside until she disappeared around the hedge.

Dinner. Great idea. *Not.*

What were you thinking?

Lauren spent the day chastising herself and making sure she didn't let on to her mother that she'd somehow invited Gabe into the inner sanctum of her house, her kitchen and her solitary life. But she'd made the offer and it was too late to back out now. Besides, he was doing her a favor looking after the dog. Dinner really was the least she could do in return. He'd helped her out, and it was her way of saying thank-you. It was nothing. Just a simple meal between neighbors.

Only, simple seemed at odds with the way her nerves rattled just thinking about it.

She stopped by the supermarket on the way home, and by the time she pulled into the driveway, it was nearly six. She jumped into the shower, dried off, applied a little makeup and changed into loose-fitting cargo pants and a red knit top. By six-thirty she was in the kitchen marinating steaks and prepping a salad. And ignoring the knot in the pit of her stomach as best she could.

The doorbell rang at exactly seven o'clock.

Jed rushed down the hallway the moment she opened the door, clearly eager to get to his food bowl in the laundry.

"Hi," she said, and stepped back.

"Hi, yourself," Gabe said as he crossed the threshold.

He closed the door, and she didn't linger. Instead, she pivoted on her heels and headed back to the kitchen. By the time she'd made her way back behind the countertop, he was by the door, watching her. She looked up and met his gaze. He looked so good in his jeans and navy T-shirt, her breath stuck in her throat. She noticed a tattoo braid that encircled one biceps peeking out from the edge of his sleeve. She'd never liked ink much, but it suited him. It was sexy. Everything about Gabe was sexy. His broad shoulders, black hair, dazzling blue eyes… The combination was devastating. And dangerous.

Be immune to sexy.

He moved and rested against the door frame, crossing his arms, and Lauren was instantly absorbed by the image it evoked.

"You know, you really shouldn't look at me like that," he said, and Lauren quickly realized she'd been caught staring. Or ogling. "I might start thinking you aren't serious about that vow of yours."

Her skin warmed. "Don't flatter yourself."

His lips curled at the edges. "I never do."

"I don't believe that for a second."

"Then what do you believe, Lauren?" he asked, and met her gaze.

"I don't know what you mean."

His stare was unwavering. "I think you do."

"You're talking about what you overheard at the wedding?" She shrugged as casually as she could manage. "I thought we'd agreed not to talk about that."

He half smiled. "Did we? You said you wanted a passionless relationship."

Her breath caught. She didn't want to talk about that with him. Not when her pulse was racing so erratically. She remembered how he knew her secrets. He knew what she wanted. "Yes," she replied and hated that it tasted like a lie. "Passion is overrated."

"Do you think?" he asked quietly, his intense gaze locked with hers. "And chemistry?"

"Even more overrated."

"That's a handy line when you're in denial."

She tried but couldn't drag her gaze away. "I'm not in denial," she insisted. "About…anything."

About you. That was what she meant. And he knew it, too.

"Good," he said, almost as though he was trying to convince himself. "Shall I open this?" he asked, and gestured to the wine bottle he carried.

Lauren nodded and grabbed two glasses and a corkscrew from the cupboard, laying them on the counter. "How do you like your steak?"

"Medium rare," he replied. "You?"

She shrugged. "Same. Did Jed behave himself today? No disasters? No sacrificial sneakers?"

He grinned and grabbed the corkscrew. "It was moderately better than the last time."

She laughed softly. "He's usually very civilized when Cameron is around."

"He's pining," Gabe said, and popped the cork. "Missing the people he loves most. It's natural he would."

Lauren nodded. "You're right. And it's only for a few more days. I heard from Cameron's house sitter this morning, and she's flying back into Bellandale on Sunday afternoon."

He passed her a glass of wine, and Lauren's fingers tingled when they briefly touched his. If he noticed, he didn't show it. "How long have you lived here?" he asked.

"Just over a year."

"It's...nice. My sister, Bianca, would love it," he said easily and rested against the countertop. "She's into decorating."

Lauren pulled a couple of plates from the cupboard. "Do you have one of those large Italian-American families?"

"There are four of us. Aaron is thirty five and the eldest. He's divorced and has twin four-year-old boys. And then there's me, three years younger." He grinned a little. "Then Luca, who's thirty and married to his IT job, and Bianca, who is twenty-six and the baby of the family."

She nodded. "And your parents?"

"There's only my mom," he explained, watching her with such blistering intensity, Lauren found it hard to concentrate on preparing their meal. "My dad died fifteen years ago."

Her expression softened. "I'm sorry. Were you close?"

"Very."

She nodded again. "What did he—"

"Lung cancer."

The awful words hung in the air between them, and an old pain jabbed between her ribs. She pushed the memory off as quickly as it came.

"I'm sorry," she said gently. "I feel very lucky to still have both my parents."

"And there's only you and Cameron?" he asked.

"Yes," she replied. "And he's actually my half brother. Our mother married my dad when he was three years old. I would have loved a sister, though. I mean, we're really close, but a big family would be wonderful."

His gaze absorbed hers. "You want children?"

She nodded. "I always thought I'd like to have three kids."

He raised a brow. "With Mr. No-Passion?"

A smile tugged at his mouth, and Lauren couldn't stop her lips from creasing into a tiny grin. "Maybe. Hopefully. One day."

He looked at her oddly, as if he wanted to have an opinion about it but was holding his tongue. When he finally spoke, he surprised her. "You'll make a good mom."

"I… Thank you." The air crackled, and she avoided eye contact by feigning a deep interest in the salad she'd prepared. When he spoke again, she looked up.

"Need any help?" he asked, and took both wineglasses to the table.

"No," she replied and plated the food quickly. "I'm nearly done. Take a seat."

A minute later, she placed the plates on the table and sat down. For one crazy second she thought…no, *imagined*… that the mood between them felt a little like a date. *A first date.*

Stupid. They were neighbors. Acquaintances. Nothing more. So what if he was the most attractive man she'd ever met? Attraction hadn't done her any favors in the past. She'd been attracted to James, and that had ended badly for them both. This would be the same. And anything more than attraction was out of the question.

"So did you have a similar job in California?" she asked, determined to steer the conversation away from herself.

"Not really," he replied vaguely and picked up the utensils. "I worked as a lifeguard part-time at Huntington Beach, near where I lived."

"Cameron said the place has never run so smoothly. Do you enjoy the work?" she asked.

"Yeah…sure," he replied casually. "I like the beach," he

said, and when she raised a brow indicating she wanted him to elaborate, he continued. "And I get to teach a few classes, lifeguard on the weekends and juggle paperwork during the week." He shrugged. "It's not exactly rocket science."

She was itching to ask him more questions. Cameron had told her he was clearly overqualified for the role at the surf club. She knew he didn't talk about himself much, and that suited her fine. Most of the time. But tonight she was interested. As much as warning bells pealed, she wanted to know more about him. She wanted to know what made him tick. She wanted to know why he'd moved his life from California to Crystal Point.

"Don't you miss your old life? Your friends, your family?"

He looked up. "Of course."

"I could never leave my family like that," she said, and knew it sounded like a judgment. She shrugged and sighed a little. "I mean, I'd miss them too much to be away for too long."

If it was a dig, he ignored it. Because he was so mesmerized by her sheer loveliness, Gabe couldn't look away. He shouldn't have come around. He shouldn't have thought he could spend an evening with Lauren and not get caught up in the desire that thrummed through his blood. She was tempting. And he was…tempted.

"You really are quite beautiful."

The words were out before he could stop them. She fumbled with her cutlery, and the steak portion on the end of her fork fell back onto the plate. He watched as she pressed her fingertips against her mouth and discreetly wiped away a little sauce.

"Um…thank you. I guess."

Gabe rested back in his chair. "You don't sound convinced."

"That I'm beautiful?" She shrugged. "I've never really thought I was. Attractive, perhaps."

"No," he said quietly. "You're beautiful."

She grabbed her drink. "Are you coming on to me?" she asked bluntly.

Gabe chuckled. "No."

She met his gaze. "Because I'm not your type?"

"I'm not coming on to you because you're exactly my type."

Heat filled the space between them, and a sudden surge of blinding attraction clung to the air. But it was best to get it out in the open. He wanted her. And he was pretty sure the feeling was reciprocated.

"Is that because of what I said about you…you know… at the wedding?"

"You mean when you told your friends you've thought about me naked?"

Color quickly flamed her pale cheeks. "Is that what I said?"

"Yes."

She shrugged and smiled a little. "Well, since you were there and heard the whole conversation, there's no point denying it."

Gabe laughed. He liked that about her. She wasn't serious all the time. Even without her natural beauty, she had an energy and humor that fascinated him. For a moment, Gabe wished he could wind the clock forward, to a time in the future when he could guarantee any promises or commitment he might want to make. But he couldn't. And wishes were for fools.

He pushed some words out. "I guess not. Your friends don't seem to approve of your plans, though."

"They don't," she said, and sipped some wine. "But they support me, so that's all that matters. You know how family and friends can get sometimes…as if they know what's best, regardless of how a person might feel about it."

Gabe knew exactly. "You don't like weddings much?"

Her eyes widened. "Sure I do. Weddings are…my life."

"Really?"

She looked at him. "Well, maybe not my life. My job, at least."

He heard hesitation in her voice. "But?"

Her shoulders dropped. "Oh, you know, pretending the fairy tale exists on a day-in-and-day-out basis can be monotonous." She shook herself and picked up the cutlery again. "Sorry, I don't normally complain about it. But you're…" She stopped and looked at him. "Even though a week ago I was convinced you were simply another ridiculously handsome but conceited jerk, you're surprisingly… easy to talk to."

A good bedside manner is essential….

How many times had he heard that?

Gabe shook off the guilt between his shoulder blades. "Oh, I can be just as much of a jerk as the next guy."

She laughed, and the sound echoed around the room. "Well, thanks for the warning."

He placed his elbows on the table. "Don't thank me. I said I wouldn't make a pass. I didn't say it would be easy."

Her cheeks bloomed with color. "Oh, because I'm—"

"Because you're Commitment 101."

"And you're not?" she queried.

"Exactly."

"Have you ever been tempted? Or close?" she asked and pushed her barely eaten meal aside.

"Once," he replied and took a drink. "It didn't work out."

She stared at him, as if she was trying to figure out why. But she never would. He didn't talk about it. Ever. She took a second, swallowed hard and then spoke. "Did you love her?"

"It didn't work out," he said again, a whole lot quicker than he would have liked. "I guess there's your answer."

Her brows arched. "So you didn't love her? Not even a little bit?"

Gabe's mouth twisted. "I didn't realize there was such a thing as being a little bit in love. I cared for her, sure. But like I said, we didn't work out. There's no great mystery to it."

He wasn't about to tell Lauren that she was right—he hadn't really loved his ex-girlfriend. He'd done her a favor by letting her go. He was sure of it. And besides, Mona hadn't put up much resistance. Once she'd known she had an out clause, she'd left their relationship as quickly as she could.

Lauren bit her bottom lip, watching him. "So you got burned?"

He shrugged. "Not exactly."

"Then what, exactly?" she asked.

"We split up," he replied. "We went our separate ways. Neither of us was heartbroken."

"Which leaves you where?" Her eyes were full of questions. "Working at the surf club and having casual relationships and sex with women who are equally uninterested in commitment?"

"Ah...I suppose."

"Well, that sounds...like fun."

Not.

That was what she was thinking. Shallow and meaningless and hollow. Gabe thought so, too...even though he'd drilled himself to accept his present and future. But he suddenly lost his appetite.

"It is what it is," he said, and pushed back in his seat. "I'm not looking for...anything."

She watched him, her brown eyes darkening. "I've always believed that we're all looking for something...love or sex, belonging, companionship. Or maybe something more complicated, like peace of mind…or even isolation."

Which one are you looking for?

That was the question in her words. Gabe shrugged a shoulder casually. She was so close to the truth. "Is that why your marriage didn't work out?" he asked, shifting the focus back to her. "Because you wanted different things?"

She gripped her wineglass. "My marriage failed because my husband and I had nothing between us but fleeting physical attraction. Which isn't enough," she added.

It explained why she wanted a passionless relationship… sort of. "And now you're looking for more?" he asked. "Or maybe less?"

"Sometimes less *is* more," she replied. "Which is why I'm determined to think with my head next time…and not my—" she paused, smiling "—libido."

Gabe tensed. Thinking of *her* libido didn't do his any favors. "Or your heart?"

She smiled. "Precisely," she said.

He remembered what his cousin had said to him the night before. She'd lost someone. She'd lost love and settled for sex. The fact that she now wanted a middle road made perfect sense. "Someone did get it, though?"

Her gaze was unwavering. "You mean my heart? Yes. Someone did."

"Who was he?"

Silence stretched between them. He shouldn't have asked. He shouldn't want to know. The more he knew, the harder it would be to stay away from her.

"My first love. My only love, I guess."

She said the words so quietly and with such raw honesty, his insides contracted. He didn't want to hear any more. "You don't have to—"

"His name was Tim," she said, cutting him off. "We met

in college. I was nineteen and studying business. He was across the hall in engineering. We fell in love. A few years later we got engaged. And then…"

Gabe knew what was coming, but he asked anyway. "And then, what?"

She drew in a sharp breath. "And then he died."

"Was it an accident?"

She shook her head. "No. He was sick."

Sick…

Gabe's stomach churned uneasily, and he forced the next words out. "What kind of illness did he have?"

"Primary glioblastoma," she replied. "It's a—"

"I know what it is," he said quickly and pushed his chair back some more.

Brain tumor…

An aggressive, unforgiving kind of cancer that usually left a patient with months to live rather than years. It was all he needed to hear. It was time to go. He needed to finish eating and leave.

"I'm sorry," Gabe said, and spent the following few minutes pretending interest in his food. Even though he felt sick to his stomach. He pushed the meal around on the plate, finished his wine and declined the coffee she offered to make.

"I need to get going," he said as soon as he felt it was polite to do so, and stood.

"Oh…sure." She got to her feet. "Thanks again for looking after Jed."

"No problem. Thanks for dinner."

Once they reached the front door, he lingered for a moment. He liked her. A lot. She was sweet and warm and funny and so damned sexy, he could barely think of anything other than kissing her perfectly bowed mouth. He wanted Lauren in his bed more than he'd wanted anything for a long time.

But he wouldn't pursue it.

She'd lost the man she'd loved to cancer.

And he'd bet his boots it wasn't a road she'd ever want to travel again.

He needed to forget all about Lauren. And fast.

Chapter Four

Spending the evening with Gabe confirmed for Lauren that since her divorce, she'd gone into a kind of lazy hibernation. She'd quit volunteering at the surf club, rarely joined her mother for the tai chi classes she'd always loved and avoided socializing regularly with anyone other than her two closest friends. It hadn't been a deliberate pulling away, more like a reluctance to go out and put on her happy face.

That needed to change.

Lauren knew if she was going to find someone to share her life with, she actually needed to start having a real *life*.

But that real life didn't include her sexy neighbor.

On Friday night she went to the movies with Cassie and Mary-Jayne, stayed out afterward for coffee and cake and got home by ten.

There was a light on next door. Lauren ignored the fluttering in her stomach and headed inside. As soon as she'd crossed the threshold, she heard Jed's whining. Minutes later she discovered her great plan of leaving him locked in the laundry was not such a great plan. It was, in fact, a disaster. He'd somehow chewed a hole in the back door, and his big head was now stuck between the timbers. Lauren groaned, cursed her brother under her breath for a few seconds and then attempted to pull the dog free. But he was lodged. His neck was wedged around the cracked timber, and she didn't have the strength to pull him free.

Surprisingly, the dopey dog was in good spirits, and she patted him for a moment before she grabbed her phone. She could call her father? Or perhaps Mary-Jayne might be able to help?

Just get some backbone and go and ask Gabe.

She reassured the dog for a little while longer before she walked next door. The porch light flickered and she sucked in a breath and knocked.

Gabe looked surprised to see her on his doorstep.

"Lauren?" He rested against the door frame. "What's up?"

He wore faded jeans that were splattered with paint, and an old gray T-shirt. There was also paint in his hair and on his cheek. She wanted to smile, thinking how gorgeous he looked, but didn't. Instead, she put on a serious face.

"I need help."

He straightened. "What's wrong?"

"It might be better if you just see for yourself."

He was across the threshold in seconds. "Are you okay?"

"I'm fine. Jed, on the other hand..."

"What's he done now?" Gabe asked as they headed down the steps.

"Like I said, you need to see this for yourself."

A minute later they were in her house. They moved to the laundry and were facing Jed's bouncing rear end. And Gabe was laughing loudly. Really loudly. In fact, he was laughing so hard he doubled over and gripped the washing machine.

"It's really not that funny," she said crossly and planted her hands on her hips. "He could be hurt."

"He's not hurt," Gabe said, still chuckling as he moved across the small room and knelt down beside the dog. "The goofy mutt is just stuck."

"Exactly. He's wedged in and I can't pull him free."

He examined the door. "Do you have a hammer?"

"A hammer?"

"I need to knock a bit of this plywood out the way," he explained.

She nodded and grabbed the small toolbox under the sink. "I think there's something in here."

He opened the box, found the small hammer and got to work on the door. Jed whined a little, but Lauren placated him with pats and soothing words while Gabe made the hole large enough for the dog's head to fit back through. It took several minutes, but finally Jed was free and immediately started bounding around the small room, whipping Lauren's legs with his tail.

"Oh, that's good," she said on a relieved sigh. "Thank you."

"He looks okay," Gabe said, smiling. "But your door's not so lucky."

Lauren glanced at the door. The hole was bigger than she'd thought. "I'll need to call someone to fix it on Monday."

He nodded as he rose to his feet. "Sure. I'll board it up for you now so you'll be safe over the weekend."

Lauren's insides contracted. The way he spoke, the way he was so genuinely concerned about her, melted what was left of her resentment toward him.

Admit it...you like him.

A lot.

Too much.

"Ah—thanks," she said quietly and moved Jed out of the small room.

Gabe followed her. "Be back soon," he said as he strode down the hallway and headed out the front door.

He returned five minutes later with a large square piece of plywood, a cordless drill and a box of screws, and quickly repaired the hole. Lauren watched from her spot near the door, absorbed by the way he seemed to do everything with such effortless ease. Nothing fazed him. He was smart and resourceful and sexy and warmed the blood in her veins. Gabe made her think of everything she'd lost. And everything she was determined to avoid.

"Lauren?"

His voice jerked her back to earth. He was close. They were sharing the space in the narrow doorway, and Lauren's gaze got stuck on his chest and the way the paint-splattered T-shirt molded his chest. Her fingertips itched to reach up and touch him, to feel for herself if his body was as strong and solid as it looked. She remembered how he'd pulled her from the pool at the wedding and how his hands had felt upon her skin. It had been a long time since she'd felt a man's touch. Longer still since she'd wanted to.

Memories of Tim swirled around in her head. She'd loved him. Adored him. She'd imagined they would spend their lives together, loving one another, having children, creating memories through a long and happy marriage. But he'd never, not once, made her knees quiver and her skin burn with such blistering, scorching awareness. Even the fleeting desire she'd felt for James seemed lukewarm compared to the way Gabe made her feel. Her sex-starved body had turned traitor, taunting her…and she had to use her head to stay in control.

"I was…I was thinking…"

Her words trailed off when she looked up and met his blistering gaze. There was so much heat between them. Undeniable heat that combusted the air and made her stomach roll.

"Thinking?" he asked softly. "About what?"

Lauren willed some movement into her feet and managed to step back a little. "Your jacket," she muttered and turned on her heels and fled through the kitchen and toward the guest bedroom.

When she returned, Gabe was in the hallway, tools in hand.

"I forgot to return this," she explained and passed him the dinner jacket he'd given her the night of the wedding and which she'd since had dry-cleaned. "Thank you for lending it to me."

"No problem." He took the garment and smiled. "Well, good night."

"Ah—and thanks again for freeing Jed…. Your saving me from disaster is becoming something of a habit."

"No harm in being neighborly," he said casually.

Too casually. She knew he was as aware of her as she was of him. But they were skirting around it. Denying it.

"I guess not. Good night, Gabe."

He left, and Lauren closed the door, pressing her back against it as she let out a heavy sigh. Being around Gabe was wreaking havoc with her usual common sense. He wasn't what she wanted. Sure, she could invite him into her bed for the night. But that was all it would be. He'd called her Commitment 101, and he was right. He'd told her he didn't do serious. He didn't want a relationship. They were too different.

When she arrived at The Wedding House the following morning, her mother was there before her, as was their part-time worker, Dawn.

"You look terrible," her mother remarked, clearly taking in her paler-than-usual skin and dark smudges beneath her eyes. Lauren wasn't surprised she looked so haggard—she hadn't slept well. Instead, she'd spent the night fighting the bedsheets, dreaming old dreams, feeling an old, familiar pain that left her weary and exhausted.

"Gee—thanks," she said with a grin. "Just a little sleep deprived because of Jed, but I'll tell you about that later."

Irene smiled. "Are you heading to the surf club this afternoon? Or do you want me to go? We have to have the measurements for the stage and runway to the prop people by Monday, remember?"

She remembered. There was a fund-raiser at the surf club planned for two weeks away, and although Grace was the event organizer, Lauren volunteered to help in her sister-in-law's absence. Since she was organizing a fashion parade for the night anyway, it wasn't too much extra work liaising with the staging and entertainment people and the caterers.

"I'll go this afternoon," she said, and ignored the silly fluttering in her belly. All she had to do was measure the area for the stage and change rooms for the models. It was not as if she would be hanging around. It was not as if she had a reason to *want* to hang around.

"If you're sure," her mother said, her eyes twinkling.

Her übermatchmaking mother knew very well that Gabe might be there.

"I'm sure," she insisted. "And stop doing that."

Her mother raised both brows. "What? I just want to see my only daughter happy."

"I want to see me happy, too," Lauren said, and instructed Dawn to open the doors.

"I'm concerned about you," Irene said, more seriously.

"I'm fine, Matka," she promised. "Just tired, like I said."

The models for the parade had started coming into the store for their fittings, and that morning Carmen Collins crossed the threshold and held court like she owned the world. They'd gone to school together, and the self-

proclaimed society princess made it her business to insult
Lauren at every opportunity. But the other woman knew
people with deep pockets, and since that was what the fund-
raiser was about, Lauren bit her tongue and flattered Carmen about the tight-fitting, plum-colored satin gown she
was wearing in the parade.

"I do adore this color," Carmen purred and ran her hands
over her hips. "So are you modeling in the parade?"

"No," Lauren replied and saw her mother's raised brows
from the corner of her eye. "I'll be too busy with the show."

"Pity," Carmen said with a sugary laugh. "You do look
so sweet in a wedding dress."

Lauren plastered on a smile and pulled back the fitting
room drapes. "Maybe next year," she said, clinging to her
manners as though they were a life raft. "I'll have the dress
pressed and ready for the show."

The other woman left by eleven, and her mother didn't
bother to hide her dislike once Carmen was out the door.

"Can't bear that woman," Irene said, and frowned. "She
was an obnoxious teenager and hasn't improved with age."

"But she married a rich man and knows plenty of people who'll donate at the fund-raiser," Lauren reminded her
mother. "That's all that matters, right?"

Her mother huffed out a breath. "I suppose. Anyway,
we've only got three more of the models to come in for a
fitting and we're done. So off you go." She shooed Lauren
and smiled. "I'll close up."

Lauren grinned, hugged her mother, quickly changed
into gunmetal-gray cargo pants, a pink collared T-shirt and
sneakers and then headed to the Crystal Point Surf Club
& Community Center to measure the space she'd need for
the catwalk.

The holiday park was filled with campers and mobile
homes, and she drove down the bitumen road that led to the
clubhouse. Almost a year earlier, the place had been gutted

by fire, and the renovated building was bigger and better with much-improved facilities. She parked outside, grabbed her tape measure and notebook and headed through the automatic doors on the ground level.

And came to an abrupt halt.

Gabe was there.

Wet, laughing and clearly having a good time in the company of a lifeguard, a young woman who Lauren vaguely recalled was named Megan.

"Lauren?" he said as he straightened from his spot leaning against the reception desk. "What brings you here?"

She held up the tape. "Benefit stuff," she said, and tried to ignore the way the safety shirt he wore outlined every line and every muscle of his chest and shoulders at the same time as the little green-eyed monster was rearing its head.

Snap out of it.

"Do you know Megan?" he asked and came toward her. She nodded. "Hello."

"It's Mimi," the girl corrected cheerfully, showing off perfectly white teeth and a million-dollar smile to go with her athletic, tanned body. "No one calls me Megan except my parents." She laughed and gazed at Gabe a little starry-eyed. "And you." Then she turned her attention back to Lauren. "So Gabe said you might be filling in for Cameron while he's away if we get too busy. The beaches have been crazy today.... Gabe just pulled an old man in from the rip."

Lauren smiled and looked at Gabe. That explained why his clothes were wet and why he had sand on his feet. "Is the man okay?"

"Shaken up, but fine," he replied and smiled. "But I wouldn't call him old. He was probably only forty."

Perfectly toned and tanned *Mimi* laughed loudly. "Ancient," she said, and grabbed Gabe's arm, lingering a lot longer than Lauren thought appropriate. "Well, I'd better get back on patrol. See you."

She breezed out of the room with a seductive sway that Lauren couldn't have managed even if she'd wanted to.

"Do you need help with that?" Gabe asked, looking at the tape in her hand.

Lauren shook her head. "No."

"So you're organizing the benefit with Grace?"

She looked at him. "The fashion parade. Why? Are you interested in modeling?"

He laughed. "Ah, no thanks. I did promise your brother I'd help out setting up, but that's all."

Lauren placed the retractable tape at one end of the room, and when it bounced back into her hand, he walked over and held it out straight for her. "Thanks," she said, and pulled the tape out across the room.

"If you need models, perhaps Megan can help?" he suggested and came across the room.

"Mimi," she corrected extrasweetly, and placed the notebook on the desk. "And I think I have all the models we need." Lauren remained by the desk and raised a brow. "She's a little young, don't you think?"

He frowned. "No. She's a strong swimmer and a good lifeguard."

Lauren flipped the notepad open without looking at him. "That's not what I meant."

The second he realized her meaning, he laughed loudly. "She's what, nineteen? Give me *some* credit."

Lauren glanced sideways. "She's perky."

"And a teenager." He moved closer. "Why all this sudden interest in my love life?"

"I'm not interested," she defended, and shrugged as she faked writing something on the notepad. "You can do what you like. Although, everyone knows that interoffice romances can be tricky and—"

Lauren was startled when he touched her arm gently. Mesmerized, she turned to face him. Side by side, hips against the desk, there was barely a foot between them. She tilted her head back and met his eyes. His gaze traveled over her face, inspecting every feature before settling on her mouth. It was intensely erotic, and her knees quivered. The hand on her arm moved upward a little, skimming over her skin, sending jolts of electricity through her blood.

Her lips parted...waiting...anticipating...

It had been so long since she'd been kissed. Too long. And she knew *he* knew that was what she was thinking.

"I'm not going to kiss you," he said softly, his gaze still on her mouth. "Even though I want to, and it would certainly stop you talking nonsense about Megan."

"All I—"

"Shh," he said, and placed two fingertips against her lips. "Keep talking, and I *will* kiss you."

Lauren knew she had to move. Because if she didn't, sanity would be lost, and she'd fling against him and forget every promise she'd made to herself. The fleeting attraction she'd experienced the first time they'd met six months ago had morphed into heady, hot desire that was slowly becoming all she could think about.

And it's not what I want....

Mindless passion was dangerous.

And if I'm not careful, I'm going to get swept up in it all over again....

"You promised," she reminded him on a whisper. "Remember? No making passes."

"I know what I promised," he said, and rubbed his thumb against her jaw. "I did warn you I could be a jerk, though."

Lauren took a deep breath. "You know what I want."

"And you seem to be of a mind to tell me what I want," he said, still touching her lips. "Which is not, I might add, a teenager with a silly crush."

"She's more woman than teenager, and—"

He groaned. "You really do talk too much."

If the automatic doors hadn't whooshed open, Lauren was certain he would have kissed her as if there was no tomorrow. And she would have kissed him back. Vow or not.

"Gabe," Mimi's squeaky voice called frantically from the doorway. "I need your help."

He dropped his hand and stepped back. "What's wrong?"

"There's a lady on the beach who's had a fall, and I think she might have broken her ankle."

Gabe moved away from her and grabbed the first-aid bag. "Okay...show me where."

He was out the door in a flash, and Lauren took a few seconds to get her feet to move and follow. By the time she reached the first crest of the sandbank, Gabe was already attending to the elderly woman. He was crouched at her side, one hand on her shoulder and asking her questions while Mimi unzipped the first-aid bag.

Lauren moved closer to assist. And took about ten seconds to realize that Gabe didn't need her help. He knew exactly what he was doing.

It wasn't broken, but his patient, Faye, had a severe sprain and probably tendon damage, and as he wrapped her ankle, he instructed Megan to call for the ambulance. The woman was well into her eighties, and her tender skin was bruising quickly. She needed X-rays and the type of painkillers he couldn't administer.

Gabe wrapped her in a thermal blanket to ensure she didn't go into shock and stayed with her and her equally elderly husband until the paramedics arrived. The beach was busy, and he sent Megan back onto patrol and remained with the couple...excruciatingly aware that Lauren was watching his every move.

Once the ambulance arrived, it was about a fifteen-minute process to get Faye from the beach and safely tucked inside the vehicle. Her husband chose to travel in the ambulance, and Gabe accepted the old man's car keys for safekeeping and was told their grandson would be along to collect the car within the hour.

His shift was over by three o'clock, but he lingered for a while to ensure the remaining bathers were staying between the boundary flags, as the water was choppy. Megan took off for home, and Gabe headed back to the clubhouse to lock up. He found Lauren in his office, sitting at the desk and writing in her notebook. He watched her for a moment, thinking that an hour earlier, he'd been on the brink of kissing her. It would have been a big mistake. Definitely.

"Did you get your work done?" he asked when he came into the room.

"Yes," she replied and collected her things together.

"I gather this benefit is important?"

She nodded. "It will raise money for the Big Brothers Big Sisters program. Cameron said you've been working with the program, too."

"A little," he replied, reluctant to tell her any more. Like the fact he volunteered his time to help coach an under-twelve's swimming and lifesaving team twice a week.

"You and Cameron put me to shame."

"How so?"

She shrugged and stood. "He's always been community focused. Not…self-focused. You're like that, too, otherwise you wouldn't be doing this job you're clearly overqualified for, or do things like volunteering with the kids from the Big Brothers program."

Discomfiture raced across his skin. So she knew. "It's nothing, really. Just a couple of hours twice a week."

"It's more than most people do," she qualified. "More than I do."

"You're helping with the benefit," he reminded her. "Raising money for the program is something important."

She shrugged again. "I guess. You know, you were

amazing with that elderly lady. Cameron was right about you…you have a talent for the first-aid side of things in this job."

Gabe's insides crunched. He could have told her the truth in that moment. He could have told her that she was right. But that it wasn't talent. It was experience. He could have told her that for ten years he'd worked as a doctor in the E.R. at the finest hospital in Huntington Beach. But if he did, she'd want to know why he left.

Why I quit…

And how did he tell her that? One truth would snowball into another.

And Gabe wasn't ready.

He wasn't ready to admit that an innocent woman and her baby had died on his watch.

Chapter Five

Lauren dropped Jed off at her brother's house on Sunday afternoon. The house sitter was back and would be in residence until Cameron and Grace returned from their honeymoon. It was past five by the time she got home, and by then she only had half an hour to shower, change and prepare an array of snacks for the girls' night she was having with Cassie and Mary-Jayne.

It was impossible to *not* notice the bright yellow car parked at the entrance of Gabe's driveway.

She'd spotted the same vehicle outside the surf club. Megan's car. Obviously.

So what? He can do what he likes.

But Lauren had to force back the swell of jealousy burning through her veins.

She'd never *done* jealous. Not even with Tim. And she certainly wasn't going to waste time thinking about her neighbor and the perky *Mimi* doing *whatever* over the hedge.

When her friends arrived, Lauren headed through the front door to greet them and immediately heard a woman laughing. She noticed that Megan and Gabe were now outside and standing by the yellow car, clearly enjoying one another's company. And her stupid, rotten and completely unjustified jealousy returned with a vengeance. She willed it away with all the strength she could muster. When Cassie and Mary-Jayne reached the porch steps, they must have noticed the scowl on her face, because they both had raised brows and wide smiles on their faces.

"Trouble in paradise?" Cassie asked and walked up the steps.

Her friends knew what had happened at the wedding. They'd called it fate. Kismet. *Providence*. The fact he'd moved in next door simply added fuel to their combined romantic foolishness.

Mary-Jayne blew out a low whistle. "That's some serious competition you have there."

Of course she meant Megan. Young, perky, chirpy... Everything she wasn't. Lauren's scowl deepened. Her friends were teasing, but she felt the sting right through to her bones. For Gabe's no-commitment, casual-sex-only lifestyle, the effervescent Megan was no doubt perfect. She was pretty and uncomplicated. She probably wasn't haunted by memories of a lost love. She almost certainly wasn't looking to settle down and raise a family. So, perfect.

"Glaring at her over the hedge won't make her turn to stone, you know," Mary-Jayne said, and grinned.

Worse luck.

She jabbed her friend playfully in the ribs. "I need a drink," Lauren said as she turned on her heels and followed the two other women back inside.

Ten minutes later they were settled in the living room, a tray of snacks on the coffee table and a glass of wine in hand. Except for Cassie, who made do with sparkling grape juice.

"Have you heard from Doug?" Lauren asked her pregnant friend as she settled back in the sofa. "Has he warmed to the idea of the baby?"

The fact that Cassie's much older soldier boyfriend hadn't taken the news of her pregnancy very well had become a regularly talked about subject between them. It had been a month since Cassie had told him the news about the baby, and Lauren was concerned for her friend.

"He said we needed to talk about it," Cassie explained, her eyes shadowy. "I know he'll come around and consider this baby a blessing. But I don't want to distract him while he's on a mission."

"He's a total jerk," M.J. said bluntly, and tossed her mass of dark curls. "You know that, right?"

Lauren quickly took the middle ground. Something she often had to do. Cassie was a calm, sweet-natured woman who avoided confrontation and drama, while effervescent M.J. attracted it like a bee to a flower. Lauren figured she was somewhere in between. As different as they were, she knew they shared one common trait—unfailing loyalty to one another and their friendship.

"Perhaps we shouldn't judge him too quickly," she said, and ignored M.J.'s scowl.

"He should be judged," M.J. said, and grunted. "Do you even know where he is at the moment?"

Cassie shook her head. "Not really."

Lauren tapped Cassie's arm. "His brother might know. Perhaps you should—"

"Tanner's in South Dakota," Cassie said quietly. "And he and Doug rarely talk. Besides, Doug will come around. You'll see."

Lauren hoped so, for her friend's sake. And if not, she'd

be there to support Cassie, just as her friends had rallied around her when she'd needed them.

Cassie smiled. "So let's talk about you, not me. What's been going on between you and Mr. Gorgeous from next door?"

"Nothing," Lauren replied, and drank some wine. She wasn't about to tell them about the near-miss kiss at the surf club the previous afternoon. They'd be all over that information in a second. It wasn't as though she really wanted to exclude them. She knew they worried about her. They'd been her rocks after Tim died. And then again when James had walked out. But they didn't really understand her determination to avoid those kinds of feelings…even though they supported her. But Gabe was a complication she didn't need to discuss with her friends. The more time she spent with him, the less she felt she knew.

And she had to get him out of her system once and for all.

Only, she had no idea how she was supposed to do that when he had a habit of invading her thoughts…and her dreams.

It was ironic how much Gabe had come to avoid hospitals. At one time, the four walls of Huntington Beach's largest health-care facility had been his life. But then everything changed. Funny how some lingering fatigue and a small lump in his armpit could so quickly alter his fate.

Biopsy…cancer…surgery…chemo…radiation therapy…

The disease had been caught early, and with a bit of luck he'd been assured of a long life, but that didn't mean he could avoid the necessary follow-up examinations every six months. The specialist asked the usual invasive questions on his visit—questions he'd never considered invasive until he'd been on the other end of the conversation. Being a cancer patient had certainly altered his perspective on having the right kind of bedside manner. If he did decide to practice medicine again, he would do it with a renewed respect for what the sick endured.

If...

Gabe missed his career more than he'd ever imagined he would. Becoming a doctor had been his dream since he was twelve years old, and getting into medical school had been the realization of years of study and hard work. But things changed. Life changed.

And then one arrogant decision had altered everything.

He'd gone back to work too soon. Everyone around him said so. His family. His colleagues. His oncologist. But after a bad reaction to the treatment and medication, and after six weeks in bed chucking his guts up, he'd had enough. He was determined to reclaim his life and return to the job he loved.

Two weeks later a young mother and her baby were dead.

Perhaps technically not his fault, but he knew in his heart that the blame lay at his feet. Nauseated and tired from that day's round of treatment, Gabe had left a second-year resident alone in the trauma room for a few minutes and headed for the bathroom. While he was gone, a patient had been brought into the E.R. and the young doctor didn't have the experience to handle the emergency. The young woman, who was seven months pregnant, had hemorrhaged, and both she and her unborn child died.

Plagued by guilt, after the inquiry, an undercurrent of uncertainty had shadowed him and he'd stuck it out for another month before he bailed on his career, his friends and his family.

His life as he knew it.

And Crystal Point was as far away from all that as he could get.

It was a place where he could wrap himself in anonymity. A place where he could forget the past and not feel defined by his illness or the tragedy of that terrible night in the E.R.

"Gabe?"

He stopped beneath the wide doorway of the specialist's rooms. Lauren stood a few feet away. Discomfort crawled along his skin. She was the last person he'd expected to see. And the last person he wanted to see outside the specialist's office.

"Hello," he said quietly, and wondered how to make his getaway.

She came to a stop in front of him. "What are you doing here?"

He took a second and considered all the things he wouldn't say. "What are *you* doing here?"

She frowned. "My friend Cassie works on reception in Radiology. I'm meeting her and Mary-Jayne for lunch."

She had a friend who worked at the hospital? One who might recognize him when he came in for testing? His discomfort turned into an all-out need to get away from her as quickly as possible before she asked more questions. Before she worked things out.

"I have to go," he said, and stepped sideways.

Her hand unexpectedly wrapped around his forearm and she said his name. Her touch was like a cattle brand against his skin, and Gabe fought the impulse to shake her off. Being this close didn't help his determination to stay away from her.

"Is everything okay?" she asked, and glanced up at the signage above his head. The word *oncology* stuck out like a beacon.

Any second now she's going to figure it out.

Dread licked along his spine. The thought of Lauren looking at him with sympathy or pity or something worse cut through to his bones. "Everything's fine."

She didn't look convinced. But Gabe wasn't about to

start spilling his guts. He wanted to get out of there as fast as he could.

She half smiled and then spoke. "I'm just surprised to see you here. Are you visiting someone or—"

"Last I looked I wasn't obligated to inform you of my movements."

His unkind words lingered in the space between them, and he wanted to snatch them back immediately. Even though he knew it was better this way. For them both. He knew she was struggling with the attraction between them, just like he was. He knew she wanted someone different... someone who could give her the picket-fence life she craved. And that wasn't him. She'd lost the man she'd loved to cancer. Of course she wouldn't want to risk that again.

"I'm...sorry," she said quietly. "I shouldn't have asked. I was only—"

"Forget it, Lauren," Gabe said sharply, and saw her wince as he pulled his arm away. "And I...I didn't mean to snap at you." The elevator nearby dinged and opened, and he wanted to dive inside. "I have to go. I'll see you later."

Gabe moved away and stepped through the doors. Away from her. And away from the questions in her eyes.

But by the end of the week, he was so wound up he felt as though he needed to run a marathon to get her out of his system. He needed to, though...because he liked being around her too much. He liked the soft sound of her voice and the sweet scent of her perfume. He liked the way she chewed her bottom lip when she was deep in thought. He liked how her eyes darkened to a deep caramel when she was annoyed, and wondered how they'd look if she was aroused. He wondered lots of things...but *nothing* could happen.

She'd lost her fiancé to cancer...making it the red flag of the century.

And Gabe had no intention of getting seriously involved

with anyone. Not until he was sure he could offer that some-one a real future. He had a five-year plan. If he stayed cancer-free for five years, he'd consider a serious relation-ship. Maybe even marriage. Until then, Gabe knew what he had to do. He had to steer clear of commitment. He had to steer clear of Lauren.

Cameron returned from his honeymoon midweek and stopped by the surf club Saturday morning just as Gabe was finishing off first aid to a pair of siblings who'd be-come entangled with a jellyfish. He reassured their con-cerned mother her children would be fine, and then joined his friend at the clubhouse.

"Busy morning?" Cameron asked, looking tanned and relaxed from his weeks in the Mediterranean, as he flaked into a chair.

"The usual summer holiday nonsense," he replied. "Sun-burn and dehydration mostly."

Cameron nodded. "Thanks for helping my sister out with Jed. She told me what happened to her door."

Gabe shrugged. "No problem," he said quickly, and tried to ignore the way his pulse sped up. He didn't want to talk to his friend about Lauren. He didn't want to *think* about Lauren. "Gotta get back to work."

Cameron stood and shook his head. "Thanks again. And don't forget to swing by my folks' house tonight, around six," he reminded him. "My beautiful wife is trying out her newly learned Greek cooking skills in my mother's kitchen, so it should be mighty interesting."

Gabe experienced an unexpected twinge of envy. His friend looked ridiculously happy. Cameron had the same dopey expression on his face that Scott permanently car-ried these days. He was pretty sure he'd never looked like that. Not even when he'd been with Mona.

"Sure," he said, thinking the last thing he wanted to do

was spend an evening at Lauren's parents' home, because he knew Lauren would be there, too. "See you then."

When he got home that afternoon, he changed into jeans and a T-shirt and started painting the main bedroom. It kept him busy until five-thirty. Then he showered, dressed and grabbed his car keys.

When he reversed out of the yard, he realized that Lauren was doing the same thing. Their vehicles pulled up alongside one another at the end of their driveways. He stopped, as did she. Their windows rolled down simultaneously.

"Hi," she said. "Are you going to my—"

"Yes," he said, cutting her off.

"My brother mentioned you were coming. Probably foolish to take both cars?"

She was right. He should have offered to drive her. But he hadn't seen her since their meeting at the hospital. He'd behaved badly. Rudely. Gabe nodded. "Probably."

"So…" Her voice trailed. "Yours or mine?"

Gabe sucked in some air. "I'll drive."

Her mouth twisted. "Be back in a minute."

He watched as she moved her car back up the driveway, got out and came around the passenger side of his Jeep. When she got in, the flowery scent of her perfume hit his senses. She buckled up and settled her gaze to the front.

"Ready?" he asked.

"Yes."

He backed the car onto the road and then came to a halt. He had something to say to her. "Lauren, I want to apologize again for being so dismissive the other day." He invented an excuse. "I was late for an appointment and—"

She waved a hand. "Like you said, not my business."

Gabe was tempted to apologize again. But he didn't. He nodded instead. "Okay."

She flashed him a brief look. "Just so you know, when we turn up together my mother is going to think it's a date."

"It's not, though," he said, and drove down the street. "Right?"

"Right," she replied.

Gabe reconsidered going to the Jakowskis'. He didn't want Lauren's mother getting any ideas. Or Cameron. Whatever he was feeling for Lauren, he had to get it under control. And fast.

Lauren knew the moment she walked into her mother's kitchen that she was going to get the third degree. Irene had greeted them at the door, explained that Cameron had been called into work and would be joining them later and quickly shuffled Gabe toward the games room to hang out with her father.

Her mother ushered Lauren directly into the kitchen. Grace was there, standing behind the wide granite counter, looking radiant. Her new sister-in-law was exceptionally beautiful. In the past, she'd always considered the other woman frosty and a little unfriendly, but Lauren had warmed toward Grace since it was clear her brother was crazy in love with her, and she with him.

Lauren stepped in beside Grace and began topping her mother's signature baked lemon cheesecake, a task she'd done countless times. Her sister-in-law remained silent, but her mother wasn't going to be held back.

"It's nice that Gabe could join us this evening. He really is quite handsome," Irene said as she busied herself pulling salad items from the refrigerator. "Don't you think? And such a lovely accent."

Lauren's gaze flicked up briefly. *"Matka,"* she warned, and half smiled. "Don't."

But she knew her mother wouldn't give up. "Just stating the obvious."

"His ancestors are Roman gods," Lauren said, and grinned. "So of course he looks good."

Irene laughed softly. "That's the spirit…indulge my matchmaking efforts."

"Well, there's little point fighting it," Lauren said with a sigh. "Even though you're wasting your time in this case."

"Do you think?" her mother inquired, still grinning as she grabbed a tray of appetizers. "Don't be too quick to say no, darling. He might just be the best of both worlds," Irene said, and smiled. "When you're done decorating that cake, can you grab the big tureen from the cabinet in the front living room?"

Lauren smiled. "Sure," she replied, and waited until her mother left the room before speaking to her sister-in-law. "See what I have to put up with?"

"She just cares about you," Grace replied, and covered the potato dish she'd prepared. "And he seems…nice."

He is nice. That was the problem. He was also sexy and gorgeous and not the *settle-down* kind of man she was looking for. He'd said as much. And she'd had nice before. Tim had been the nicest, most sincere man she'd ever known. Even James had been nice in his own charming, flirtatious way. The kind of nice she wanted now didn't come with a handsome face and the ability to shoot her libido up like a rocket.

The best of both worlds…

What exactly did her mother mean? That Gabe was attractive, charming, funny and smart and just what any sensible woman would call the *perfect package?*

Too perfect. No one was without flaws. Secrets.

Lauren placed the cheesecake in the refrigerator and excused herself. The big living room at the front of the house was rarely used. It housed her mother's treasures, like the twin glass lamps that had been in their family for four generations, and the cabinet of exquisite crockery and dinnerware. Lauren stopped by the mantelpiece and stared at the family photographs lining the shelf. There were more pictures on the long cabinet at the other end of the room. Her mother loved taking pictures.

She fingered the edge of one frame and her insides crunched. It was a snapshot of herself and Tim. He looked so relaxed and cheerful in the photo. They were smiling, pressed close together, his blond hair flopping over his forehead. Had he lived, he would have been soon celebrating his thirtieth birthday. She looked at his face again. It was Lauren's favorite picture of him. Memories surged through her. Memories of love. And regret. And…anger. But she quickly pushed the feeling away. Anger had no place in her heart. Not when it came to Tim.

"You looked happy."

Lauren swiveled on her heels. Gabe stood behind her. Engrossed in her memories, she hadn't heard his approach. "Sorry?"

"In the picture," he said, and stepped closer. "You looked happy together."

"We were," she said, intensely conscious of his closeness. "That's…Tim," she explained softly and pointed to the photograph. "He was always happy. Even when he was facing the worst of it, somehow he never lost his sense of humor."

Gabe's eyes darkened. "Did he pass away quickly?"

She nodded. "In the end…yes. He died just a few weeks before we were due to be married."

"And then you married someone else?"

"Not quite two years later," she replied and immediately wondered why she was admitting such things to him. "It was a big mistake."

Gabe nodded a little. "Because you didn't love him?"

"Exactly," she said, and sucked in a short breath.

"There must have been something that made you marry him?"

Lauren's skin grew hotter. "Sex."

His blistering gaze was unwavering. "That's all?"

"I'd had love," she admitted, so aware of his closeness she could barely breathe. "And I'd lost it. When I met James, I thought attraction would be enough."

"But it wasn't?"

She sighed. "No."

"And now you don't want that, either?" he asked.

Lauren raised a shoulder. "I don't expect anyone to understand."

"Actually," he said quietly. "I do. You lost the love of your life, then settled for something that left you empty, and now you want to find that no-risk, no-hurt, middle road."

Middle road? Could he read her mind? "That's right. I married my ex-husband after only knowing him for three months. It was a foolish impulse and one I regret…for his sake and mine."

Gabe looked at the mantelpiece. "Which explains why there are no pictures of him."

"My mother was never a fan of James," she said, and felt his scrutiny through to her bones. "Once we divorced, the wedding pictures came down." Lauren looked down to her feet and then back up to his gaze. "Ah…what are you doing in here? I thought you were out on the back patio with my dad."

"I was," he replied, and grinned fractionally. "But your mother sent me on a mercy dash to help you carry some kind of heavy dish."

Lauren rolled her eyes and pointed to the tureen in the cabinet. "My mother is meddling."

He smiled, like he knew exactly what she meant. "To what end?"

Lauren raised a shoulder. "Can't you guess? I told you she'd think this was a date."

His gaze widened. "Should I be worried?"

She laughed a little. "That my mother has her sights set on you? Probably."

Gabe laughed, too, and the sound warmed her right through to the blood in her veins. He was so...likable. So gorgeous. And it scared her. With James, she'd jumped in, libido first, uncaring of the consequences. Still grieving the loss of the man she'd loved, Lauren had found temporary solace in arms that had soon left her feeling empty and alone. Although she'd thought him good-looking and charming, she'd realized soon after they'd married that they had very little in common. But the attraction she had for Gabe was different. The more time she spent with him, the less superficial it felt. Which put her more at risk.

"I shall consider myself warned," he said, and chuckled.

Lauren walked toward the cabinet and opened the door. "Thanks for being so understanding," she said, still grinning.

"I, too, have a meddling, albeit well-meaning mother who wants to see me...shall we say, *settled.* So I understand your position."

For a second, she wondered what else they had in common. He clearly came from a close family, as she did. "Doesn't she know you're not interested in commitment?"

His gaze locked with hers. "I don't think she quite believes me."

Lauren's breath caught. "Have you..."

"Have I what?"

She shrugged, trying to be casual but churning inside. "Have you changed your mind about that?"

Lauren couldn't believe she'd asked the question. And couldn't believe she wanted to know. Her elbow touched his arm and the contact sent heat shooting across her skin.

She should have pulled away. But Lauren remained where she was, immobilized by the connection simmering between them.

"No," he said after a long stretch of silence. "I haven't."

Of course, it was what she needed to hear. Gabe wasn't what she wanted. Because he made her feel too much. He made her question the choice she'd made to remain celibate until she found someone to share her life with. He didn't want what she wanted.

He's all wrong for me....

Even though being beside him, alone and in the solitude of the big room, seemed so unbelievably normal, she was tempted to lean closer and invite him to kiss her. His gaze shifted from her eyes to her mouth, and Lauren sucked in a shallow breath. Her lips parted slightly and he watched with such searing intensity, her knees threatened to give way. There was heat between them, the kind that came before a kiss. The kind of heat that might lead to something more.

"Gabe..." She said his name on a sigh.

"We would be crazy to start something," he warned, unmoving and clearly reading her thoughts.

"I know," she agreed softly.

Crazy or not, she was strangely unsurprised when he took hold of her hand and gently rubbed his thumb along her palm. He was still watching her, still looking at her mouth.

"Do you have any idea how much I want to kiss you right now?"

She shivered at his question, despite the warmth racing across her skin. Lauren nodded, feeling the heat between them rise up a notch. "Do you have any idea how much I want you to kiss me right now?"

His hand wrapped around hers. She was staring up, waiting, thinking about how she hadn't been kissed for such a long time. And thinking how Gabe had somehow, in a matter of weeks, become the one man whose kiss she longed for.

Chapter Six

Gabe could have kissed her right then, right there. He could have lost himself in the softness of her lips and sweet taste of her mouth. He could have forgotten about his determination to keep away from her and give in to the desire he experienced whenever she was near. And he would have. But a loud crash followed by an equally loud shout pushed them apart immediately. The dish from the china cabinet was quickly forgotten as they both hurried from the room.

When they reached the kitchen, he saw there was glass and water on the floor and also a pile of tattered flowers. Lauren's father was sitting on the ground, knees half-curled to his chest.

"Dad!" Lauren gasped as she rushed to his side.

Irene and Grace came through the doorway and stood worriedly behind Gabe as he quickly moved between them to settle beside the older man. Franciszek Jakowski was holding up a seriously bleeding hand, and Gabe quickly snatched up a tea towel from the countertop and wrapped it around his palm.

"I knocked the darn vase off the counter," Franciszek explained as Gabe hauled him to his feet. "Cut myself when I fell."

"Can you walk?" Gabe asked, knowing he needed to look at the wound immediately.

Franciszek winced as he put weight on his left foot. "Not so good."

He looked at Lauren. "Hold your father's hand up to help with the bleeding, and I'll get him to a chair."

She did as he asked, and Gabe hooked an arm around the other man's shoulder and soon got him settled onto the kitchen chair. Blood streamed down his arm and splattered on Gabe's shirt. He undid the towel and examined Franciszek's hand. The cut was deep and would need stitches. Irene disappeared and quickly returned with a first-aid kit. Gabe cleaned and dressed the wound, conscious of the scrutiny of the three women hovering close by. Within minutes, he also had Franciszek's left ankle wrapped with an elastic bandage.

"The cut definitely needs stitches," he said, and wiped his hands on a cloth Lauren passed him. "And it looks like you've only sprained your ankle, but an X-ray wouldn't hurt just to be sure."

Irene extolled her gratitude and was on the telephone immediately, making an appointment to see their local doctor within the next half hour.

"I'll drive you," Lauren volunteered, but her mother quickly vetoed that idea.

"Grace can drive us," she said, and looked toward her daughter-in-law, who nodded instantly. "You can stay and clean up. And I need you to keep an eye on dinner. We won't be too long."

"That's for sure," Franciszek agreed cheerfully, although Gabe was pretty sure the older man was in considerable pain. He patted Gabe's shoulder. "Thanks for the doctoring, son. Much appreciated."

Gabe's stomach sank. Being reminded of who he was, even though no one but his family knew the truth, hit him like a fist of shame between the shoulder blades. He glanced at Lauren and then looked away. There were questions in her eyes. Questions he had no intention of answering.

It took several minutes to get Franciszek into the car, and when Gabe returned, Lauren was in the kitchen, picking up pieces of shattered glass from the floor. She was concentrating on her task, looking shaken and pale.

"Are you okay?"

She glanced up. "Just worried about my dad."

"He'll be fine."

Her small nose wrinkled. "Thanks to you," she said as she rose to her feet and walked around the countertop. "You might want to consider switching careers."

His gut sank. "What?"

"You'd make a good paramedic," she said, and grabbed a banister brush from the cupboard beneath the sink. "You clearly have a knack for it. You know, I have a friend who's an admin in emergency services. I could probably arrange for you to—"

"No…but thank you," he said, cutting her off before she said too much about it. "Need some help with this?"

She held his gaze for a moment, and then passed him the broom. "Sure. I'll get the mop and bucket." She propped her hands on her hips and looked at his blood-stained shirt. "I'll find you something to wear and you can pop that shirt in the machine before it permanently stains. I think Cameron has some clothes in one of the guest rooms. I'll go and check."

She disappeared, and Gabe stared after her. Guilt pressed

down on his shoulders. He wanted to tell her the truth about himself. But one would lead to another and then another. And what was the point? There were already too many questions in her lovely brown eyes.

When she returned with the mop and bucket, she placed a piece of clothing on the table. "I'll finish up here. You can go and change."

He met her gaze. "Okay."

Gabe left the room and headed for the laundry. Once there, he stripped off his soiled shirt and dumped it in the washing machine. He added liquid, cranked on the start switch and rested his behind on the edge of the sink. Then he expelled a long breath.

Damn.

He wanted to kiss her so much. He wanted to touch her. He wanted to feel her against him and stroke her soft skin. He wanted to forget every promise he'd made to himself about waiting to see if his illness returned before he'd consider being in a relationship. But it wouldn't be fair to any woman. More than that, it wouldn't be fair to Lauren. He couldn't ask her to risk herself. He *wouldn't*. He'd seen firsthand what it had done to his mom when his father had battled cancer for three years. He'd watched his mom lose the light in her eyes and the spirit in her heart. He'd watched her grieve and cry and bury the man she'd loved.

And Lauren had been there, too. He'd heard the pain in her voice when she'd spoken of her lost love. It should have been enough to send him running.

She thought he'd make a good paramedic? The irony wasn't hard to miss. There were questions in her eyes, and they were questions he didn't want to answer. But if he kept doing this, if he kept being close to her, he would be forced to tell her everything.

And admitting how he'd bailed on his life and career wasn't an option.

Pull yourself together and forget her.

He needed to leave. And he would have if Lauren hadn't chosen that moment to walk into the laundry room.

When Lauren crossed the threshold, she stopped dead in her tracks. Gabe stood by the sink in the small room with the fresh shirt in his hands. And naked from the waist up. He turned to face her.

It had been so long since she'd been this close to a man's bare skin. And because it was Gabe, he was thoroughly mesmerizing, as she'd known he would be. She'd known his skin would look like satin stretched over steel and that his broad shoulders and arms would be well defined and muscular. The smattering of dark hair on his chest tapered down in a line and disappeared into the low waistband of his jeans, and Lauren's breath caught in her throat.

His gaze instantly met hers, and she didn't miss the darkening blue eyes and faint pulse beating in his cheek. Somehow, she moved closer, and when Lauren finally found her voice, they were barely feet apart.

She dropped the bucket and mop. "I…I'm sorry…I didn't realize you were still in here."

Heat swirled between them, coiling around the small room, and she couldn't have moved even if she wanted to. She tried to avert her gaze. Tried and failed. He had such smooth skin, and her fingers itched with the sudden longing to reach out and touch him.

"You…" Her voice cracked, and she swallowed. "You were right with what you said before. We'd be…crazy…to start something…to start imagining we could…"

Her words trailed off, and still he stared at her, holding her gaze with a hypnotic power she'd never experienced before. Color spotted her cheeks, and she quickly turned and made for the doorway. Only she couldn't step forward because Gabe's hands came out and gently grasped her shoulders. She swallowed hard as he moved in close behind her and said her name in that soft, sexy way she was becoming so used to. The heat from his body seared through her thin shirt, and Lauren's temperature quickly spiked. His hands moved down her arms and linked with hers. She felt his soft breath near her nape, and his chest pressed intimately against her shoulders.

His arms came around her and Lauren pushed back. One hand rested on her hip, the other he placed on her rib cage. The heat between them ramped up and created a swirling energy in the small room. Her head dropped back, and she let out a heavy sigh as his fingertips trailed patterns across the shirt. It was an intensely erotic moment, and she wanted to turn in his arms and push against him. She wanted his kiss, his touch, his heat and everything else. She wanted him to plunder her mouth over and over and then more. Flesh against flesh, sweat against sweat. She wanted his body over her, around her, inside her. She wanted *him*... and not only his body. Lauren tilted her head, inviting him to touch the delicate skin at the base of her neck with his mouth. But he didn't. Instead, Gabe continued to touch her rib cage with skillful, seductive fingers, never going too high and barely teasing the underside of her breasts.

She could feel him hard against her. He was aroused and not hiding the fact. Lauren moved her arms back and planted her hands on his thighs. She dug her nails against the denim and urged him closer. His touch was so incredibly erotic, and she groaned low in her throat. Finally, he kissed her nape, softly, gently, and electricity shimmered across her skin.

"Lauren," he whispered against her ear as his mouth trailed upward. "I'm aching to make love to you."

Lauren managed a vague nod and was about to turn in his arms and beg him to kiss her and make love to her when she heard a door slam. The front door. Seconds later, she heard her brother's familiar voice calling out a greeting.

Gabe released her gently and she stepped forward, dragging air through her lungs. "I should go."

"Good idea," he said softly as he grabbed the shirt and pulled it quickly over his head. "I should probably stay here for a minute."

She nodded and willed some serious movement into her legs and was back in the main hallway seconds later. Cameron, dressed in his regulation police-officer uniform, greeted her with a brief hug and ruffled her hair.

"Hey, kid…what's happening?" he asked once they were in the kitchen and saw the pan of broken glass on the countertop.

She quickly filled him in about their father's mishap, and once she was done, he immediately called Grace. Her brother was still on the phone when Gabe walked into the room. Her body still hummed with memories of his touch, and their gaze connected instantly. If Cameron hadn't turned up, she was sure they'd be making love that very minute. And it would have been a big mistake. When the moment was over, there would be regret and recrimination, and she'd hate herself for being so weak.

When her brother ended his call, he explained that their father was being triaged, and that they'd be home as soon as he was released. In fact, they returned close to an hour and a half later. By then, Lauren had shuffled the men out of the kitchen and finished preparing dinner.

It turned out that Gabe was right. Her father had needed stitches for his hand, and his foot was only sprained. By the time they settled her dad at the head of the table, crutches to one side, it was nearly nine o'clock. Lauren was seated next to Gabe and felt his closeness as if it was a cloak draped across her shoulders.

Once dinner was over, she headed back to the kitchen

with Grace and began cleaning up. Gabe and her brother joined them soon after, and Grace tossed a tea towel to each of them.

"Idle hands," her sister-in-law said, and grinned when Cameron complained. "Get to work."

Lauren laughed and dunked her hands into a sink full of soapy water. Like with everything he did, Gabe ignored Cameron's whining and attended the task with an effortless charm that had both Lauren and Grace smiling. It would, she decided, be much better if he had the charisma of a rock. But no such luck. Aside from the insane chemistry that throbbed between them, Lauren liked him so much it was becoming impossible to imagine she could simply dismiss her growing feelings. Sexual attraction was one thing, emotional attraction another thing altogether. It was also hard to dismiss how her mother, Grace and even her brother watched their interaction with subtle, yet keen interest.

By the time they left, it was past eleven o'clock, and then a quarter past the hour when Gabe pulled his truck into his driveway. She got out, and he quickly came around the side of the vehicle.

"Well, thanks for the lift," she said, and tucked her tote under her arm.

He touched her elbow. "I'll see you to your door."

"There's no need," she said quickly.

"Come on," he said, and began walking down the driveway, ignoring her protest.

Lauren followed and stepped in beside him as they rounded the hedge that separated their front lawns. He opened the gate and stood aside to let her pass. By the time she'd walked up the path and onto the small porch, she was so acutely aware of him she could barely hold her keys steady.

Open the door. Say good-night. Get inside. Easy.

Lauren slid the key in the screen door and propped it

open with her elbow while she unlocked the front door. "Um…thanks again," she said, and turned on her heels. "And thanks for what you did for my dad. I'm glad you were there to—"

"Lauren?"

She stilled, clutching her tote, hoping he wouldn't come closer. Praying he wouldn't kiss her. "We…we need to forget what happened tonight," she said in a voice that rattled in her throat. "We agreed it would be crazy to—"

"Nothing really happened," he said, cutting her off. "Did it?"

Lauren took a breath. "Well, what *almost* happened. I've made a vow, a promise to myself…and it's a promise I intend to keep. And I'm never going to find what I want if I get drawn deeper into this…this attraction I have for you. We both know it won't go anywhere other than your bed, and I'm not prepared to settle for just sex. Not again."

He didn't move. But he stared at her. He stared so deeply, so intensely, she could barely breathe. The small porch and dim light overhead created extreme intimacy. If she took one tiny step she would be pressed against him.

"You're right," he said, and moved back a little. "You shouldn't settle for sex. You should find that middle road you want, Lauren, with someone who can give you the relationship you deserve."

Then he was gone. Down the steps and through the gate and quickly out of view. Lauren stayed where she was for several minutes. Her chest was pounding. Her stomach was churning. Her head was spinning.

And her heart was in serious danger.

Gabe knew he was right to leave Lauren alone. He hadn't seen her all week. Deliberately. He left for work earlier than she did and returned home before her small car pulled into the driveway each afternoon. Not seeing her helped. A lot. Or more like a little. Or not at all.

Unfortunately, not seeing her seemed to put him in a bad mood.

Something his cousin took pleasure in pointing out on Thursday afternoon when Gabe dropped by the B and B.

"You know, you'll never get laid if you don't ask her out," Scott said with a wide grin, and passed him a beer.

"Shut up," he said, and cranked the lid off.

His cousin laughed. "Hah. Sucker. Just admit your five-year plan is stupid and that you're crazy about Lauren."

Gabe gripped the bottle. "I know what I'm doing."

"Sure you do," Scott shot back. "You're hibernating like a bear because you don't want to admit you like her. That's why your mom has been calling my mom and my mom has been calling me. You haven't been taking any calls from your family for the past two weeks."

"They worry too much," he remarked, and shrugged. "They think I'm going to relapse and die a horrible death. And maybe I will. All I know is I don't want to put anyone in the middle of that. Not anyone. Not Lauren."

"Maybe you should let her decide that for herself."

"Will you just…" Gabe paused, ignored the curse teetering on the end of his tongue and drank some more beer. "Stop talking."

Scott shrugged. "Just trying to see my best friend happy."

"I'm happy enough," he shot back. "So lay off."

His cousin laughed, clearly unperturbed by his bad temper. "You know, not every woman is going to run for the hills if you get sick again."

"Mona didn't run," Gabe reminded the other man. "I broke it off with her."

Scott shrugged again. "Another example of you needing to control everything, right?"

Tired of the same old argument, Gabe finished his beer and stood. "I have to bail."

"Hot date?"

Gabe grabbed his keys off the table. "A wall that won't paint itself."

"Sounds riveting," Scott said drily. "Renovating that house won't keep you warm at night, old buddy."

His cousin was right, but he had no intention of admitting that. He took off and was home within a few minutes. Once he'd dropped his keys on the hall stand, he rounded out his shoulders. Pressure cramped his back, and he let out a long breath. He needed to burn off some of the tension clinging to his skin. There was easily over an hour of sunlight left, so he changed into his running gear and headed off down the street.

Gabe reached The Parade quickly. The long road stretched out in front of him. He crossed the wide grassy verge and headed for the pathway leading to the beach in one direction and to the north end of the small town to the other. He vetoed the beach and headed left, striding out at an even pace and covering the ground quickly. It was quiet at this end of town. Without the holiday park, surf club and kiosk there was only a scattering of new homes, and the waterfront was more rock than sand. He spotted a pair of snorkelers preparing to dive close to the bank and waved as another runner jogged past.

Up ahead, he spotted someone sitting alone on one of the many bench seats that were placed along the line of the pathway. It was Lauren. He'd recognize her blond hair anywhere. He slowed his pace and considered turning around. But he kept moving, slowing only when she was about twenty feet away. She was looking out toward the ocean, deep in thought, hands crossed in her lap. An odd feeling pressed into his chest. As though he suddenly couldn't get enough air in his lungs. God, she was beautiful. He stopped a few feet from the seat and said her name.

Her head turned immediately. "Oh, hi."

She was paler than usual. Sadder. The tightness in his chest amplified tenfold.

He stopped closer. "Are you okay?"

"Sure," she said quietly, unmoving.

Gabe wasn't convinced. He moved around the bench and sat down beside her. "I'm not buying. What's up?"

"Nothing," she insisted.

"It's four-thirty on a Thursday afternoon. You're not at the store," he said pointedly. "You're sitting here alone staring out at the sea."

She shrugged a little. "I'm just thinking."

He knew that. "About what?"

She drew in a shallow breath. "Tim."

Of course. Her lost love. "I'm sorry, I shouldn't have—"

"It's his birthday," she said quietly, and turned her gaze back to the ocean. "I always come here on this day. It's where he proposed to me."

Gabe immediately felt like he was intruding on an intensely private moment. Big-time. He got up to leave, but her hand came out and touched his arm.

"It's okay," she said, her voice so quiet and strained it made his insides twinge. "I could probably use the company."

"Do you usually?" he asked. "Have company, I mean?"

She shook her head and dropped her hand. "Not usually."

Gabe crossed his arms to avoid the sudden urge to hold her. He looked out at the sea. "You still miss him?"

"Yes," she said on a sigh. "He was one of the kindest people I've ever known. We never argued. Never had a cross word. Well, that is until he…"

Her words trailed, and Gabe glanced sideways. "Until he what?"

She shrugged again. "Until he was dying," she said, so softly he could barely hear. "It sounds strange to even say such a thing. But I didn't find out he was sick until a few weeks before the wedding."

"His illness progressed that quickly?"

She shook her head. "Not exactly. He knew for over six months. He just didn't tell me."

Gabe's stomach sank. But he understood the other man's motives. The unrelenting guilt. The unwanted pity. Gabe knew those feelings well. "He was trying to protect you."

"So he said. But all I felt was…angry."

The way she spoke, the way her voice cracked and echoed with such heavy pain made Gabe wonder if it was the first time she'd admitted it out loud. Her next words confirmed it.

"Sorry," she said quietly. "I don't ever whine about this stuff to anyone. And I don't mean to criticize Tim. He was a good man. The best. When we met we clicked straight-away. We were friends for a few months, and then we fell in love. Even though it wasn't fireworks and insane chem-istry and all that kind of thing."

"But it was what you wanted?" Gabe asked quietly, his heart pounding.

"Yes," she replied. "But then he was gone…and I was alone."

Gabe uncrossed his arms and grasped her hand, hold-ing it tightly within his own. She didn't pull away. She didn't move. Silence stretched between them, and Gabe quickly realized that despite every intention he'd had, his attraction for Lauren had morphed into something more. Something that compelled him to offer comfort, despite the fact he had to fight the sudden umbrage coursing through his blood when she spoke about the man she'd loved. He wasn't sure how to feel about it. He wasn't sure he should even acknowledge it.

Thankfully, a few seconds later, she slid her hand from his and rested it in her lap. Gabe sucked in some air and tried to avoid thinking about how rattled he'd become by simply sitting beside her.

"You don't like being alone?"

"No," she replied. "Not really. I guess that's why I married James. And exactly why I shouldn't have." She took a long breath. "I wanted the wedding I was denied when Tim passed away."

"And did you get it?"

She nodded. "Yes. I had the same venue, the same guests and the same themed invitations." Her voice lowered. "I even wore the same dress I'd planned on wearing two years earlier."

The regret and pain in her voice was unmistakable, and Gabe remained silent.

"When I was engaged to Tim, I was so wrapped up in the idea of being married," she admitted on a heavy sigh. "Up to that point my life, my world, had been about the store and weddings and marriage and getting that happily ever after. I was so absorbed by that ideal, I didn't realize that he was sick…that he was *dying*. When he was gone, I felt lost…and I turned that grief into a kind of self-centered resentment. Afterward, I was so angry at Tim for not telling me he was ill. And then James came along, and he was handsome and charming and…and *healthy*. Suddenly, I glimpsed an opportunity to have everything I'd ever wanted."

Gabe's chest constricted. Any subconscious consideration he'd ever given to pursuing Lauren instantly disappeared. She was looking for a healthy, perfect mate. Not a cancer survivor. "But you still want that, right? Even though your marriage didn't work out?"

"I want my happily ever after," she confessed. "I want someone to curl up to at night. I want someone to make me coffee in the morning. And I really want children. It doesn't have to be wrapped up in physical attraction or even some great love story. In fact, I'd prefer it if it wasn't. It just has to be real…honest."

Her words cut him to the quick. "I hope you find what you're looking for," he said, and got to his feet. "I'll walk you home."

"That's okay," she said, and twisted her hands together. "I think I'll stay here for a while longer."

"Sure."

"And, Gabe," she said as he moved to turn away. "Thanks for listening. I needed a friend today."

He nodded. "Okay."

On the run back home, Gabe could think of only one thing. Lauren had needed a friend. The thing was, he didn't want to be her friend. He wanted more. Much more. And he couldn't have it.

Not with his past illness shadowing him like an albatross.

He was broken physically. She was broken emotionally.

And he was stunned to realize how damned lonely that suddenly made him feel.

Chapter Seven

With the benefit at the community center only hours away, Lauren really didn't have time to dwell on how she'd literally poured her heart out to Gabe just days earlier. It was better she didn't. Better...but almost impossible. Her dreams had been plagued by memories of all she'd lost. Of Tim. And more. She dreamed about Gabe, too. Dreams that kept her tossing and turning for hours. Dreams that made her wake up feeling lethargic and uneasy.

But she had to forget Gabe for the moment. Tonight was about the benefit. Her sister-in-law had done an amazing job organizing everything. It was a black-tie event, catered by the best restaurant in Bellandale. On the lawn outside the building, a huge marquee had been set up to accommodate a silent auction of items ranging from art to fashion and jewelry and a variety of vacation destinations. Under a separate marquee, there were tables and chairs set out for dinner, and a dance floor. There was also a band in place to provide entertainment. Inside the building, the runway was decorated and ready for the models to begin the fashion parade. Lauren stayed behind the scenes, ensuring hair and makeup were on track before the models slipped into their gowns. She'd also changed into a gown—a stunning strapless silk chiffon dress in pale champagne. It was shorter at the front, exposing her legs to just above the knees and then molded tightly over her bust and waist, flaring off down her hips in countless ruffled tiers that swished as she walked. She'd ordered the gown months ago and had never had occasion to wear it. Other than Cameron's recent wedding, it had been too long since she'd dressed up. Too long since she'd felt like making an effort. But tonight was special. The money raised would help several children's charities, including the Big Brothers Big Sisters program that was so important to her brother.

She hadn't seen Gabe but knew he had been there earlier, helping out with the marquees and the staging setup. Avoiding him was her best option. Avoiding him made it possible to function normally. Avoiding him was what she needed to do.

"Lauren?"

She was alone in the foyer of the community center. She'd been checking the stage and working out the music cues with the DJ, who'd since disappeared. The models were upstairs; so were Mary-Jayne and Cassie, as they'd volunteered to help with the gown changes.

Lauren turned on her high heels. Gabe stood by the door. He wore a suit, probably the same one he'd worn to her brother's wedding, and he looked so gorgeous, she had to swallow hard to keep a gasp from leaving her throat.

"Need any help here?" he asked.

Her brows came up. "Changed your mind about strutting on the catwalk?"

He laughed. "Not a chance. But I hear you roped my cousin, Scott, into it."

"Not me," she said, and placed her iPad onto the stage. "He's Mary-Jayne's brother-in-law, so she did all the convincing."

Gabe's gaze rolled over her. "You should be modeling tonight…you look beautiful."

She shrugged. "What? This old thing," she said, and laughed softly. "Thanks. You know, you don't look so bad yourself."

He grinned in that sexy, lopsided way she'd become used to. "So, need any help?" he asked again.

Lauren shook her head. "I don't think so. Grace has everything under control. She's *very* organized."

He chuckled. "You mean the consummate control freak? Yeah, I kinda figured."

Lauren relaxed her shoulders. "Well, it's good to have someone like that at the helm for this kind of event. Actually, I…"

"You…?" he prompted when her words trailed.

"Oh…nothing…I was just thinking how I should apologize for the other day."

"No need," he said quietly.

"It's only that I don't usually talk about those things. It probably sounded like I was blaming Tim for dying. I wasn't," Lauren assured him, unsure why she needed to explain herself. But she did. "Sometimes…sometimes the grief gets in the way."

His eyes darkened and he nodded as if he understood. It struck her as odd how he could do that. It was as though he knew, somehow, the depth and breadth of the pain in her heart.

"I remember how my mom was after my dad died," he said quietly. "I don't think she ever really recovered."

"Sometimes I feel like that," she said. "I feel as if the pain will never ease, that I'll be grieving him forever. And then…and then there are times when I can't remember the sound of his voice or the touch of his hand." She stopped, immediately embarrassed that she'd said so much. "I don't know why I do that," she admitted. "I don't know why I say this stuff to you. It's not like we're…" She stopped again as color rose up her neck. "The truth is, I'm very confused with how I should feel about you."

"You shouldn't be," he said softly. "We're neighbors. Friends. That's all."

If she hadn't believed he was saying it to put her at ease, Lauren might have been offended. She drew in a long breath then slowly let it out. "After what happened at my parents' house the other night, I think we're both kidding ourselves if we believe that."

"What *almost* happened," he reminded her. "There's no point getting worked up over something that didn't happen, is there?"

Annoyance traveled up her spine. He thought she was overreacting? Imagining more between them than there actually was? She pressed her lips together for a second and gave her growing irritation a chance to pass. It didn't. "Sure. You're right. There's no point. Now, if you don't mind, I have to finish getting ready for the parade."

He didn't budge. "You're angry?"

"I'm busy," she said hotly.

As she went to move past him, one of his arms came up to bar the doorway. "Wait a minute."

Lauren pressed her back against the doorjamb. He was close. Too close. "No. I have to—"

"I'm trying to make this easy for you," he said, cutting her off.

Lauren's gaze narrowed. "I think you're trying to make this easy for yourself."

He moved, and his other arm came up and trapped her in the doorway. "Maybe I am," he admitted softly. "Maybe I'm just crazy scared of you."

Scared? She wouldn't have pegged Gabe to be a man scared of anything. Especially not her. "I don't understand what you—"

"Sure you do," he said, and moved closer. "You feel it, too. Don't you know I can barely keep my hands off you?"

Lauren had to tilt her head to meet his gaze. "So it's just about attraction?" she managed to say in a whisper. "Just…sex."

Their faces were close, and his eyes looked even bluer. Lauren sucked in a shaky breath, feeling the heat rise between them against her will. She wanted to run. She wanted to stay. She wanted to lock the door and strip off her dress and tear the clothes from his body and fall down onto the carpet and make love with him over and over. She wanted him like she'd never wanted any man before.

"I wish it was," he said, and inched closer until their mouths were almost touching. "I wish I didn't like spending time with you. I wish I didn't keep thinking about you every damned minute I'm awake, and could stop dreaming about you every time I go to sleep."

The frustration in his voice was both fascinating and insulting. He wanted her but resented that he did. Thinking of his struggle ramped up her temperature. And it made her mad, too.

"Sorry for the inconvenience," she said with way more bravado than she actually felt.

"Are you?"

She glared, defiant. "You're an ass, Gabe. Right now I wish I'd never met you."

He didn't believe it. Nor did she. He stared at her mouth. Lauren knew he was going to kiss her. And she knew *he knew* she wanted him, too. There was no denying it. No way to hide the desire churning between them.

"My vow…" Her words trailed as she struggled for her good sense. "I promised myself I'd wait until—"

"Forget your vow," he said, cutting off her protest. "Just for right now, stop being so sensible."

A soft sound rattled in her throat, and Gabe drew her closer, wrapping his arms around her as he claimed her lips in a soft, seductive and excruciatingly sweet kiss. She went willingly, pressing her hands to his chest, and she felt his heart thunder beneath her palm. His mouth slanted over hers, teasing, asking and then gently taking. Lauren parted her lips a little as the pressure altered and the kiss deepened. Everything about his kiss, his touch, was mesmerizing, and Lauren's fingertips traveled up his chest and clutched his shoulders. He was solid and strong and everything her yearning body had been longing for. When he touched her bare skin where the dress dipped at the back, she instinctively pressed against him, wanting more, needing more. He gently explored her mouth with his tongue, drawing her deeper into his own, making her forget every coherent thought she possessed.

"Hey, Lauren, have you seen the—" Cassie's voice cut through the moment like a bucket of cold water. Gabe dragged his mouth from hers and released her just as Cassie came into view, emerging through the open doorway on the other side of the room. "Oh, gosh! Sorry."

Gabe stepped back, his breathing a little uneven. He stared at her, through her, into a place she never imagined she'd ever let any man into again. "Good luck with the show," he finally said to Lauren, and slipped through the doorway.

She watched him disappear then took a deep breath and faced her friend. Cassie's eyes were wide and curious. "Did you need me for something?"

Cassie grinned. "Ah, the models are getting restless. Especially Carmen Collins. I said you'd come upstairs and give them a pep talk before the parade starts."

"Sure," Lauren said, and grabbed her iPad.

Cassie cleared her throat. "Sorry about that…I didn't mean to interrupt. But the door was open and—"

Lauren raised a hand. "Please, don't apologize. I shouldn't have let it happen."

"Why not?" her friend asked. "You're single. He's single. You're awesome. He's gorgeous. You like him. He *clearly* likes you. You're friends. Neighbors. Sounds perfect."

Lauren's brows shot up. "Have you been watching *When Harry Met Sally* or *Love Actually* again?"

"Don't disregard old-fashioned romance so easily," Cassie said, and grinned.

"I don't," Lauren said. "But you know that's not what I'm looking for." *Gabe's not what I'm looking for.* But her lips still tingled. Her skin still felt hot where he'd touched her. Lauren ignored the feelings and smiled toward her friend. "Come on, let's get the models ready."

The fashion parade was a success. And Lauren was so busy for the next four hours that she didn't have a chance to think about Gabe. Or talk to him. Or remember his kiss.

The models did a splendid job, and by the time the last gown had been paraded up and down the catwalk and the entire cast returned for one encore lap, Lauren was exhausted. Her mother was on hand passing out business cards, and made several bridal-fitting appointments for the following week.

The silent auction was also a hit, and Lauren put a modest bid on a vacation up north and was outdone by her brother. Dinner was served underneath the huge marquee, and thankfully, she wasn't seated at Gabe's table. He was with Scott and Evie and some of Evie's family, while she spent the evening at a table with her brother and parents. Grace was a fabulous emcee and the auction raised thousands of much-needed dollars.

By the time dessert was served, several couples had taken to the dance floor. Lauren turned to Cassie, who was seated beside her, and immediately took note of her friend's pale complexion.

"You know, you don't look the best."

Cassie shrugged one shoulder and drank some water. "It's nothing. I'm a little tired. It's just baby hormones."

Lauren frowned. "Are you sure?"

"Positive."

She was about to get started on her dessert when she noticed someone standing behind her. Lauren knew instinctively it was Gabe. He lightly touched her bare shoulder, and the sensation set her skin on fire.

"Dance with me, Lauren?"

She looked up and met his gaze, ignoring how Cassie bumped her leg under the table. "I really shouldn't leave Cassie alone."

"I'll be fine," her friend, the traitor, assured them. "Go ahead. I insist."

He held out his hand. She took it and got to her feet. He led her to the dance floor and drew her into his arms. The woodsy scent of his cologne immediately assailed her senses and she drew in a shuddering breath. His broad shoulders seemed like such a safe haven, and she was almost tempted to imagine for one foolish moment that they were *her* safe place. Hers alone. Where no one could intrude. The place she'd been searching for. But that was a silly fantasy. She knew the rules. She'd made them. She wanted commitment and he didn't.

Like with everything he did, he moved with an easygoing confidence, and Lauren followed his lead when the music suddenly slowed to a ballad.

"You can dance," she said, and relaxed a little.

"I'm half Italian," he replied against her ear, as though that was all the explanation he needed to offer.

She couldn't help smiling. "Are you one of those men who is good at everything?"

He pulled back a little and Lauren looked up. His mouth twisted. "I guess I'll let you judge that for yourself."

His words wound up her spine like a seductive caress. Suddenly, she sensed they weren't talking about dancing. With the beat of the music between them and the memory of their kiss still hovering on her lips, Lauren was drawn into the depths of his dazzling blue eyes. As a lover, she imagined, he'd be passionate and tender and probably a whole lot of fun. Of course, she'd never know. But still…a little fantasy never hurt anyone.

"I'm sorry about before," he said, and held her close.

He regretted their kiss? "Sure. Forget about it. I have."

His breath sharpened. "I meant that it was hardly the place to start something like that. I hadn't planned on kissing you for the first time while two hundred people were within watching distance."

"So you *planned* on kissing me at some point?"

"After what happened at your brother's wedding, and all the time we've spent together since, I really don't think we could have avoided it."

Her brother's wedding? Was he referring to what he'd overheard her say to her friends? How she'd thought about him naked? Conceited jerk. "You're not irresistible, you know."

"I'm not?" he queried, and rested a hand on her hip.

Lauren could feel him smile as her forehead shadowed his chin. "No."

He chuckled. "So I guess that means you won't want me to kiss you again?"

Her belly fluttered. "Exactly. You have to remember that we want different things."

"That's right. You're still looking for Mr. Reliable?"

"Yes. And not Mr. Roll-in-the-Hay."

"Too bad for me, then," he said, still smiling. "Incidentally, have I told you how beautiful you look tonight?"

"You mentioned it."

Lauren couldn't help smiling. Their banter was flirty and harmless. Nothing more would happen unless she wanted it to. Gabe was charming and sexy, but he also oozed integrity. And she might have been tempted to sleep with him. If she didn't like him. But she did like him. A lot. Too much. And with her heart well and truly on the line, a night in his bed wouldn't be worth the risk, despite how much she wanted it.

"You're easily the most beautiful woman here tonight."

It was a nice line, even if she did think he was being overly generous. The song ended and Lauren pulled back a little. "Thank you for the dance."

"My pleasure."

As he walked her back to her table, Lauren was very aware that her mother was watching them. She could almost see Irene's mind working in overdrive. Cassie wasn't at the table, and she immediately asked after her friend.

"I think she went inside to collect her bag," her mother explained, and then patted the vacant seat, inviting Gabe to sit down.

"Be back in a minute," Lauren said, and walked from the marquee.

She found Cassie in the clubhouse upstairs, sitting on the small couch in the corner of the same room the models had used earlier as a dressing room. There were rails filled with gowns along one wall and shoes were scattered across the floor. Her friend looked up when she came through the doorway.

"Everything all right?" Lauren asked.

Cassie had her arms wrapped around her abdomen and grimaced. "It's nothing. I'm sure it's nothing."

Lauren's gaze moved to Cassie's thickened middle, and she walked across the room. "Are you in pain?"

"I'm fine," Cassie replied, and then clutched at her abdomen with both hands.

Suddenly, her friend looked the furthest from fine that Lauren had ever seen.

"What is it?" she asked and dropped beside the sofa. "What can I do?"

Cassie shook her head. "I don't know…I don't know what's wrong. It might be the baby."

There were tears in her friend's eyes, and Lauren quickly galvanized herself into action. Falling apart wouldn't help Cassie. "You need to see a doctor. I'll get Cameron to carry you into my car, and then I'll take you to the hospital."

She turned on her heels and headed for the door. Evie, Grace and Mary-Jayne were at the top of the stairs talking. "What is it?" Evie, the original earth mother, asked, and stepped toward the room.

"Cassie's ill."

The three women were in the room in seconds, and Evie touched Cassie's forehead with the back of her hand. "She has a temperature."

Cassie doubled over and gripped her belly. "It hurts so much. I'm scared. I don't want to lose my baby."

"It's okay, Cassie, you'll be fine. I'll ask Cameron to—"

"Grace, M.J.," Evie said quickly, and cut her off. "You'd better go and find Gabe."

Gabe?

Both women nodded and backed out of the room. Lauren waited until they'd disappeared and turned her attention back to Evie.

"Evie, I'm sure Cassie would prefer my brother to get her to the hospital."

Evie shook her head. "She needs a doctor. Right now."

"I agree. But I can't see how—"

"Lauren, Gabe *is* a doctor."

When Gabe entered the room, he spotted Lauren standing by the narrow sofa, comforting her friend. She looked at him, and his chest instantly tightened.

She knows....

Damn. But he'd known it was bound to come out eventually.

He wavered for a second before quickly turning his attention to the woman on the sofa. He asked Cassie a series of questions, such as how severe was the pain, was it constant or intermittent, was she spotting. And as Cassie quietly answered, he felt Lauren's gaze scorching the skin on the back of his neck.

It was hard to stay focused. Memories of that terrible night in the E.R. flooded his thoughts, and panic settled in his chest. *Just do it.* That night another pregnant woman had needed his help, and he'd failed her. But he couldn't fail Cassie. Not when Lauren was watching his every move. This was Lauren's closest friend. She'd be inconsolable if anything happened to her.

It was all the motivation Gabe needed to pull himself together. Instinct and experience quickly kicked in, and he asked Cassie to lie back on the sofa. He gently tilted her to her left side and asked questions about the position and intensity of the pain. He then quickly checked her abdomen. After a minute he spoke. "Okay, Cassie, I need you to relax and take a few deep breaths."

Cassie's eyes were wide with fear. "Do you think it's the baby? I don't want to lose my baby. I can't…I just can't… Not when Doug is so far—"

"You'll be okay. Both of you," he assured her and patted her arm. "We'll get you to the hospital." He turned toward Evie. "Call an ambulance. Tell them we have a patient in her second trimester with probable appendicitis."

Cassie let out a sob. "Do I need an operation?"

He nodded and squeezed her hand. "It'll be all right. You and your baby will be fine."

By the time the ambulance arrived, Gabe had Cassie prepared, and they were ready to go. Lauren volunteered to collect some of her friend's things from her home and meet them at the hospital. Gabe spoke to the paramedics as they carefully loaded Cassie onto the stretcher, and then he followed in his truck.

By the time he reached the hospital, Cassie was already being transferred to the surgical ward and was being prepped for an emergency appendectomy.

He'd been in the waiting room for about forty minutes when Lauren walked through the doorway. She'd changed into jeans and a blue shirt and carried a small overnight bag in one hand. She came to a halt when she spotted him.

"Is she in surgery?" she asked quietly.

Gabe got to his feet. "Yes. Is there someone we should call?"

"Only Doug, her boyfriend," she replied and placed the bag on the floor. "He's a soldier on tour, and I don't know how to contact him. I guess I could check the numbers stored in her phone. She doesn't have any real family of her own other than her grandfather, and he's in an aged-care home and suffers dementia. Doug has a brother in South Dakota, so I could call him if anything…I mean, if something…" Her eyes shadowed over. "If something goes wrong with Cassie or the baby."

"She'll pull through this," he said, fighting the urge to take Lauren into his arms.

"Do you know what's happening to her?" she asked coolly.

"You mean the surgery?" He drew in a breath. "They'll probably give her an epidural or spinal anesthesia as it's safer than general anesthesia."

"And the baby?"

"The safest time for a pregnant woman to have surgery

is during the second trimester. Cassie is seventeen weeks along, so she and the baby should be fine."

"Should?" Lauren's brows shot up. "Is that your professional opinion?"

It was an easy dig. "Yes."

She dropped into one of the vinyl chairs and sighed heavily. "I feel like such a fool."

"Lauren, I wanted to—"

"It's so obvious now," she said, and cut him off dismissively. "That first night when I picked up Jed and I got the splinter. And the old lady on the beach. And then when my dad sprained his ankle." She made a self-derisive sound. "How stupid I would have sounded to you, prattling on about how you'd make a good paramedic. What a great laugh you must have had at my expense."

Guilt hit him squarely between the shoulders. She had a way of making him want to tell her everything. "I wasn't laughing at you."

She met his gaze. "No? Then why all the secrecy?"

Gabe shrugged one shoulder. "It's a little complicated."

"Handy cop-out," she said, clearly unimpressed. "I thought we were…friends."

I don't know what we are. But he didn't say it. Because he didn't want to be her friend. He wanted to be more. And less. He wanted to take her to bed and make love to her over and over. He also wanted to stop thinking about her 24/7.

"I lost a patient," he said, and heard how the hollow words echoed around the small room. "So I took some time off."

Her expression seemed to soften a little. "Oh…" He could see her mind ticking over, working out a way to ask the next question. "Was it because of something you did wrong?"

"Indirectly," he replied and sat down opposite her. "It was around midnight and I'd worked ten hours straight.

I left the E.R. for a while, and when I was gone, a young woman was brought in. She was pregnant and hemorrhaging, and a second-year resident treated her. Unfortunately, the patient and her baby died."

She stared at him. "How awful."

"Yes," he said, remembering the event like it was yesterday. "It was a terrible tragedy. And one I will always regret."

"You said you weren't there at the time," she said, and frowned. "Which means it wasn't actually your fault."

Guilt pressed down. "It was. Even though I wasn't the only doctor in the E.R. that night, I was the attending physician on duty, and I should have been there when I was needed the most. A less experienced resident was forced to handle the situation and because of that, a woman and her child died."

It wasn't an easy truth to admit. And it sank low in his gut like a lead weight. It didn't matter how many times he replayed it over in his mind. He should have been there. His arrogance and self-importance had been the reason he'd failed the patient. The blame lay at his feet. And his alone. If he'd followed his own doctor's advice, he wouldn't have returned to work so quickly. Instead, he'd ignored everything and everyone and done it his own way. With fatal consequences.

Her eyes widened. "Were you sued?" she asked. "Was there some kind of malpractice suit? Is that why you quit being a doctor?"

Gabe's stomach tightened. *Quitter.* He'd called himself that over and over. But it had been easier leaving medicine than swallowing the guilt and regret he'd experienced every time he walked through the hospital corridors.

"There was an inquiry," he said, and ignored how much he wanted to haul her into his arms and feel the comfort of her touch, her kiss, her very soul. "The hospital reached a settlement with the woman's family. I wasn't implicated."

"And the other doctor?"

"She was suspended and left the hospital soon after."

Lauren twisted her hands in her lap. "Would you have saved the patient if you were there?"

Gabe took a deep breath. "I believe so."

"But you don't know for sure?"

He shrugged lightly. "Who can know anything for certain?"

Her gaze was unwavering. "But as a physician, wouldn't you be trained to deal with absolutes? Life or death. Saving a patient or *not* saving a patient. There are no shades of gray. It's one or the other, right?"

Her words cut deep, and he wanted to deny the truth in them. "I can't—"

"So tell me the truth," she said, and raised her brows. "Why did you really quit being a doctor?"

Chapter Eight

Lauren pushed aside the nagging voice in her head telling her to mind her own business. She couldn't. He was a mystery. A fascinating and infuriating enigma. She wanted to know more. She wanted to know everything.

Because…because she liked him. As hard as she'd tried *not* to, she was frantically drawn toward Gabe. The kiss they'd shared earlier that evening confirmed it. She hadn't planned on having feelings for him. But now that she had them, Lauren was curious to see where it might lead. He was attracted to her…. Perhaps it might turn into more than that. Maybe he'd reconsider his no-commitment position. Just as she'd begun to rethink her own plans for wanting a relationship based on things other than desire or love.

Love?

Oh…heavens. *I'm in big trouble.* The biggest. *Desiring. Liking. Loving.* Her once broken and tightly wrapped-up heart had somehow opened up again. And she'd let him in. Even if he didn't know it.

"I told you why," he said, and got to his feet.

Lauren watched him pace around the room. The tension in his shoulders belied the dismissive tone in his voice. "You told me you felt responsible for losing a patient that wasn't directly *your* patient. How is that your fault? How is that a reason to throw away your career?"

He stilled and stared at her for the longest time. Lauren knew she was way out of line. He would have been well within his rights to tell her to go to hell. But she knew he wouldn't. There was something in his expression that struck her deeply, a kind of uneasy vulnerability she was certain he never revealed. Not to anyone.

"Walking away from that life was one of the hardest things I've ever done," he said quietly. "I don't expect you or anyone else to understand my reasons."

Lauren drew in a shaky breath. "I'm sorry. I don't mean to sound like I'm judging you. I'm not," she assured him. "It's just that I...I guess I...care."

He didn't budge. His blue-eyed gaze was unwavering. Only the pulse in his cheek indicated that he understood her meaning.

"Then, don't," he said, and crossed his arms. "We've been through this before, Lauren. You want something else, something and someone who won't give you grief or pain or disappointment. That's not me. If you waste your heart on me, I'll break it," he said, his voice the only sound in the small room. "I won't mean to...I won't want to...but I will. I'm not the middle road you're looking for, Lauren."

Humiliation and pain clutched at her throat. But she wouldn't let him see it. "Sure. Whatever." She stood and grabbed the bag at her heels. "I'm going to check on Cassie."

She left the room as quickly as she could without looking as if she was on the run. Once she was back in the corridor, Lauren took several long gulps of air. Her nerves were rattled. Her heart felt heavy in her chest. She made her way to the cafeteria and stayed there for the next hour. She was allowed to see Cassie when she came out of surgery, but her friend was groggy and not very talkative. By the time Lauren headed home, it was past midnight.

Gabe's truck was not in the driveway, but she heard him return about twenty minutes after she did. She didn't want to think about him.

If you waste your heart on me, I'll break it....

It was warning enough. She'd already had one broken heart when she'd lost Tim. Lauren wasn't in the market for another. He'd made his feelings, or lack thereof, abundantly clear.

After a restless night where she stared at the ceiling until 3:00 a.m., on Sunday morning, Lauren headed off to the hospital. Seeing Cassie lifted her spirits.

"You look so much better today."

"Thanks," Cassie replied, and sighed.

Lauren placed the flowers she brought on the small bedside table. "When are you getting out of here?"

"Tomorrow," her friend replied. "The surgery went well, and the baby is okay."

There was a huge look of relief on Cassie's face, and Lauren smiled. "I'm so glad to hear it. Did you manage to reach Doug?"

She shook her head. "But I left a message."

Lauren could see her friend's despair. "I could try to call him. Or perhaps you should contact Tanner, and he could try to get in touch with his brother."

Cassie sighed. "I haven't spoken with Tanner since the last time he came home, which was a couple of years ago. Last I heard, he was still horse whispering in South Dakota. Doug will call me," Cassie said assuredly. "He will. I know it. I left a message and said it was important. He'll call me," she said again.

Lauren hoped so. Doug's reaction to the baby had been lukewarm at best, and she knew Cassie hadn't heard from him since.

"So," Cassie said, and grinned. "About Gabe. I think—"

"Let's not," Lauren pleaded.

"Indulge me. I'm the patient, remember?" she said, and patted her IV. "I'm guessing you didn't know he was really a doctor?" she asked. "And a pretty good one, by the way he reacted yesterday."

"I didn't know," she admitted.

"I guess he had his reasons for keeping it a secret."

Sure he did. He was emotionally unreliable and therefore unattainable. She'd get over him soon enough. For the moment, he was just a distraction, and her fledging feelings would recover. Lauren was sure of it.

It didn't help that the object of her distraction chose that moment to enter the room.

With Mary-Jayne at his side.

Of course, she knew he was acquainted with her friend. He was Scott's cousin, and Evie was Mary-Jayne's sister. Still…a little burst of resentment flooded her veins.

She met his gaze. He looked so good in jeans and a black polo shirt, and walked with the easy swagger she'd come to recognize as uniquely his. Lauren tried to smile and failed.

"Look who I found outside," Mary-Jayne announced with a big grin.

"Ladies," he said easily, and stepped into the room. "Am I interrupting?"

"Not at all," Cassie was quick to say. "I'm so glad you're here. I wanted to say thank you for yesterday."

Gabe shrugged. "No thanks necessary. As long as you're feeling better."

"Much," Cassie said, and beamed a smile. "Are they for me?" she asked of the bunch of flowers in his hand. When he nodded, her friend's smile broadened. "Daffodils are my favorite. Thank you."

Lauren fought back a surge of jealousy and drew in a deep breath. So he met Mary-Jayne in the hallway, and Cassie was a little starstruck? *It means nothing to me.* One kiss didn't amount to anything. She had no hold on him and shouldn't care that her friend might have a harmless crush on the man who'd potentially saved her and her baby. Besides, Cassie was devoted to Doug.

She hopped up from her chair and took the flowers, careful not to touch him. He said hello, and she managed to reply and then disappeared from the room in search of a vase.

"What's up with you?"

Lauren came to a halt and waited for Mary-Jayne to catch up. "Nothing."

Her friend grabbed her arm. "We met in the hall, that's all."

"I don't know what you mean."

Mary-Jayne's slanted brows rose up dramatically. "Sure you do. Dr. Gorgeous in there only has eyes for you."

"That's…that's ridiculous," Lauren spluttered. "We're just neighbors."

"You can deny it all you want, but I know what I see."

If you waste your heart on me, I'll break it….

His words came back again and sat like lead in her stomach.

The nurses happily obliged her with a vase, and when they returned to the room, Gabe was sitting beside Cassie's bed, and her friend's hand rested against his forearm. The scene looked ridiculously intimate. Resentment bubbled, and Lauren pushed it away quickly.

"I was just telling Gabe how grateful I am," Cassie said, and patted his arm one more time before she placed her hands in her lap and grinned at him. "Again."

He shrugged in a loose-shouldered way, but Lauren wasn't fooled. "I'll get going. Good to see you all."

Once he was gone, Cassie blew out a low whistle. "Boy, could you two be any more into each other and less inclined to admit it?"

Lauren colored wildly. "That's ridiculous."

"Yeah, right," Cassie said, and grinned. "I'm not the most observant person in the world, but even I can see that you have some serious feelings for him."

"And I think right about now is the time for me to leave," Lauren said gently, and grabbed her bag. She loved Cassie. But now wasn't the time to have a discussion about her feelings for Gabe. Feelings he'd made perfectly clear he didn't want and couldn't return.

"You know, I'm sure he had his reasons for not telling you he was a doctor," Cassie said, ignoring her indication to leave. "If that's what's bugging you. Some people don't like talking about themselves."

I know...I'm one of those people.

"I'll see you tomorrow. Make sure you let me know when you're leaving so I can pick you up. My mother is insisting you stay with her and my dad for a couple of days."

She hugged both her friends goodbye, and by the time Lauren arrived home, it was past midday. She got stuck into some cleaning and sorted through a few cupboards in the kitchen. It was menial, mind-numbing work that stopped her dwelling on other things. Or at least gave the impression. Later she did some admin work for the store and spent an hour in the backyard, weeding and repotting some herbs. Gabe wasn't home, and that suited her fine.

When she was done, it was well past five, and Lauren headed inside to clean up. She took a long bath and dried herself off before cozying into candy-pink shorts and matching tank shirt. She called Cassie and arranged to pick her friend up the following morning. With that done and the store organized for next day, Lauren ignored the idea of dinner and mooched around the cupboards for something sugary. Being a usually health-conscious woman, the pantry was bare of anything she could call junk, and she made do with a bag of organic dried apples.

She was sitting on the sofa, watching television with her knees propped up and dipping in for a third mouthful of apple when the doorbell rang. Lauren dropped the bag and headed up the hallway. When she opened the door and found Gabe standing on her porch, Lauren took a deep breath. He looked tired. As though he hadn't slept for twenty-four hours.

Well, too bad for him.

"What do you want?"

He had an envelope in his hand. "I got the estimate for the new fence. You said you wanted to—"

"Sure," she snapped, and held out her palm.

He placed the note in her hand. "You're under no obligation to pay half. The fence is my idea and I'd rather—"

"I said I'd pay for it," she said, cutting him off.

He threaded his fingers through his hair, and she couldn't stop thinking how mussed and sexy he looked. "Okay. If you're sure. Check out the estimate and if you agree, I'll get the contractor to start work in the next week or so."

Wonderful. A great high fence between them was exactly what she needed.

"I'll let you know," she said through tight teeth.

He nodded, shrugged a little and managed a smile. "I'll talk to you later."

He turned and took a few steps. Lauren wasn't even sure she'd spoken his name until he turned back to face her.

"Yes, Lauren?"

She pushed herself out of the doorway, and the light above her head flickered. He was a few feet away, but she could still make out every angle of his handsome face. A question burned on the edge of her tongue. Once she had her answer, she'd forget all about him.

"Why did you kiss me last night?"

The words seemed to echo around the garden, and the sound of insects chorused the silence that was suddenly between them. He took a couple of steps until he stood at the bottom of the stairs.

"If you think this is such a bad idea," she went on, getting stronger with each word. "If you believe there's nothing going on here…why did you even bother?"

He let out a heavy breath. "Because I had to know."

She shivered, even though it was warm outside. "You had to know what?"

"I had to know what your lips tasted like just one time."

Her shiver turned into a burn so hot, so rampant, Lauren thought she might pass out. She grabbed the screen door to support her weakened knees. No man had ever spoken those kinds of words to her. Tim had been sweet and a little shy. James's flirtatious nature had been obvious and overt. But Gabe was somewhere in between. Not shy. Not obvious. He was a seductive mix of reserve and calm, masculine confidence.

"And that's all it was? Just…just a single kiss?"

"What do you want me to say to you?" he shot back. "Do you need to hear that I want to kiss you again? That I want to make love to you? Of course I do. I've told you that before. I've never denied that I'm attracted to you, Lauren. You're…lovely. You're smart and beautiful and the more time I spend with you, the more I want you. But I can't give you the kind of commitment you want. Not…not right now."

Not right now?

What did that mean? A possibility popped into her head.

"Are you married?" she asked. "Or separated? Is that why you—"

"Of course not," he cut her off tersely.

"I had to ask," she said, and sighed. "You're so hot and cold, Gabe. You say one thing to me and then do another. I'm confused, and it seemed plausible."

"Well, it's not. I've had three semiserious relationships and a few one-night hookups. But I've never been married. I thought about it when I was with my last girlfriend, but we never got around to making any firm plans. In between, I was busy with my career."

"A career you then gave up?"

His expression turned blank. And she'd never wanted to read him more. But couldn't.

"I have to go," he said. "Good night."

She watched him leave and waited until he rounded the hedge before she returned inside and closed the door.

On Tuesday morning, Gabe noticed five missed calls on his cell. Two from his mom. Three from Aaron. His brother had then reverted to text messaging.

What's going on with you?

He sent one back when he arrived at work.

Nothing.

Aaron responded immediately.

Mom's worried about you. Call her.

Sure.

Gabe knew his one-word replies would irritate his interfering older brother.

Ten minutes later, he received another message.

Just do it, Gabriel.

Gabe ignored the deliberate use of his full name in his brother's message and stuffed the phone in his pocket. Well-meaning relatives with advice he could do without.

Megan arrived, and he plastered on a smile. It would be best if he kept his lousy mood to himself. No one needed to know that he was so wound up, so frustrated, he could barely string a sentence together. She had her older sister with her, a remarkably attractive girl in her mid-twenties whose name he couldn't recall but who looked him over with barely concealed approval.

The teen dumped a few books on his desk. "Thanks for these," she said chirpily.

"They helped?" he asked, and pulled another medical textbook from the desk drawer.

"Yeah," she replied. "I sit the nursing entrance exam next week."

Megan had borrowed a few of his old medical texts to help with her studying and hadn't asked why he had them. Not like Lauren would have. She'd ask. She'd want to know everything. And the damnable thing was, he'd want to tell her.

"Well, good luck," he replied. "Just drop it back when you're done with it."

Megan grabbed the book and sashayed out of the room, but her sibling hovered in the doorway, brows raised suggestively. In another time, he might have been tempted to ask for her number, to take her out and get her into bed after a few dates. But he wasn't interested in the pretty brunette with the wide smile. Gabe cursed to himself. He was so wrapped up in Lauren that nothing and no one else could shift his distraction. Nothing could ease the unexpected ache in his chest and the unrelenting tension cramping his shoulders. Kissing her had been like nothing on earth. And he wanted to feel that again. He wanted to take her in his arms and make love to her over and over and somehow forget he couldn't offer her the future she deserved.

The cell in his pocket vibrated again. It was another message from his brother.

You said you'd call. Get to it.

Gabe ignored the message and got back to work.

But by two he'd had enough, and since no one was booked in to use the upstairs rooms that afternoon, he locked up and headed home. Back at the house, there was painting to be done, drywall to replace and plaster, and the lawn needing mowing. But he ignored every chore. Instead, Gabe started unpacking some of the boxes in the spare room. The box marked Personal Items got his full attention. Gabe rummaged through the papers and soon found what he was looking for. His diploma of medicine. Still in the frame his mother had insisted upon. He looked at it, and shame hit him squarely behind the ribs.

Quitter...

Like he'd rarely allowed himself to think in the past eighteen months, Gabe wondered what would have happened had he stuck it out. What would have ensued had he ignored the guilt and regret tailing him around the hospital corridors? Would time have healed his fractured spirit? Would it have lessened the remorse? Would he have been able to practice medicine with the self-belief it demanded? Right now, he felt healthy. His last round of tests had come back clear. He was cancer-free.

Perhaps it was time to take his life back?

A first step. A giant step. But one he had to do if he was ever going to be truly happy.

Gabe shoved the diploma back in the box and resealed the lid.

He needed a run to clear his thoughts and stretch out the muscles in his back and limbs. He changed his clothes and headed out. When he returned, he showered, pulled on jeans and a T-shirt and grabbed his keys. If he wanted to take his career back, there was no time like the present to start.

He had a patient to check on.

Lauren sat on the edge of the bed in the spare room at her parents' house and chatted to her friend. It had been her bedroom once. Back then, the walls had been pink, and posters of rock gods had covered the walls. Since she'd moved out, her mother had redecorated in the more subtle tones of beige and white.

"This isn't necessary, you know, for me to stay in bed," Cassie insisted, and patted the mattress. "I feel fine."

"Good," Lauren said, and smiled. "But humor us all anyway, and rest for a few more days. You had surgery, and you need to take it easy."

Her friend had resisted coming to stay at her parents' home to recuperate. But since Lauren's dad was now retired, it meant that someone would be able to watch Cassie around the clock. Cassie meant a great deal to her family. She was like another daughter to her parents and as close to Lauren as a sister could be. She wasn't about to allow her friend to be alone.

"Okay," Cassie said, and grinned. "I'll be a model patient. As long as I know Mary-Jayne is looking after my dog, I'll relax."

"She is," Lauren told her. "I'll go and make some tea and bring it up with dinner."

"What time are your folks getting back?" Cassie asked.

Lauren checked her watch. It was just after seven. "Matka is at mah-jongg and will be back by nine-thirty, and Dad's helping Cameron supervise a bowling expedition with a group of kids from the Big Brothers program tonight. So you'll have to put up with me until then." She grinned. "But I promise I won't smother you."

Cassie chuckled. "Good. Um…I think I heard the doorbell. You might want to get that."

Lauren had heard it, too. She left the room and headed downstairs and was stunned to find Gabe on the other side of the door when she swung it back on its hinges.

"Oh…hi."

"Hey," he said, looking gorgeous beneath the overhead light. "I just stopped in to check on Cassie. I called her earlier, and she said she was here."

She did? Lauren needed to have a talk with her friend. She'd bet her boots Cassie had deliberately arranged this meeting. Her friend wasn't averse to a little matchmaking. Too bad it was pointless. "I didn't realize you had her number."

His mouth twitched. "I got it from Cameron."

"Oh, right. Well, she's upstairs…third room on the right."

Lauren turned on her heels and headed back down the hall. He could close the door. He could make his own way upstairs. She didn't want to spend any more time with him than was necessary. It was the only way she'd succeed in getting him out of her system.

But damn it if she couldn't hear them talking and laughing from her spot in the kitchen. The sound traveled down the stairway and managed to spur on her mounting jealousy and resentment.

She was about fifteen minutes into preparing dinner when she felt Gabe's presence in the room. Lauren looked up and noticed him in the doorway, arms crossed and one shoulder resting against the doorjamb.

"How does she seem?" she asked stiffly, slicing cucumber as though it was the enemy.

"Good," he replied, and pushed himself off the door frame. "Recovering well."

"So nice of you to make a house call." She turned toward the sink. "You know the way out."

But he stepped closer. "Is every conversation we have going to be a battle from now on?"

She harrumphed. "Probably. I should have stuck to my guns that night at my brother's wedding and ignored you. My life was simpler then."

"We couldn't ignore one another if we tried," he said, and was suddenly behind the counter.

"Oh, I can try," she assured him. "And I will."

He turned and rested his behind on the countertop. "I don't know what it is about you, Lauren... You make me think about things. You have a way of getting under my skin."

"Like a burr?" She wasn't going to be nice to him. Lauren finished the salad and soup she'd prepared for Cassie and placed it on a tray. "I'm going to take this upstairs. When I come back down, I'd prefer it if you weren't here."

By the time she was upstairs, her knees were wobbling so much she had to quickly place the tray on the bed. She looked at her smiling friend.

"I figure this is your doing?"

Cassie shrugged innocently. "Maybe a little. I thought it was sweet that he wanted to make sure I was okay. He's very nice. You shouldn't give up so easily."

"I'm not giving up," she said, and propped another pillow behind her friend. "I'm just not going to waste time dreaming about something that will never happen."

She lingered in the room for a few more minutes, giving Gabe plenty of time to leave. But when she returned to the kitchen, he was still there, still standing by the counter.

She heard his phone buzz.

"I think you just missed a call."

"I didn't miss it," he said, and shrugged a shoulder. "I didn't answer it."

"Girl trouble?" she inquired, hurting all over just thinking about it.

He half smiled, as though he knew she hated imagining him with some faceless woman. "My mom," he explained. "Or my brother Aaron…checking up on me."

"Do you need to be checked on?"

"They seem to think so," he said, and pushed himself off the counter.

"Well, I guess it's natural for a mother to worry when one of her kids lives on the other side of the world. I don't imagine my mother would be any different. She likes that Cameron and I both live close by. It makes her feel as though everything is right in her world. I don't think it matters how old we get…she just needs to know we're safe and happy, because that makes *her* feel safe and happy."

His gaze darkened, and he looked at her oddly. "You know, I don't think I've ever thought about it quite like that before."

Lauren's knees wobbled again. She was trying hard to stay strong and ignore him. But staring into Gabe's brilliant blue eyes wasn't helping. Hearing the seductive tone of his voice wasn't helping, either.

She shrugged. "I don't think we ever fully understand how hard it is for parents to let us live our own lives. They want to protect us from being hurt and from enduring life's disappointments. Even though it can sometimes feel like being wrapped in cotton wool and then be overprotected."

"Is that what happened to you?" he asked quietly. "After Tim died?"

Lauren nodded. "And again when my marriage ended. With Tim... I think because it happened so quickly, I was in shock. One moment I was planning my wedding, the next I was dressed in black and standing beside his grave. There was no time to prepare...to say goodbye. I was so mad at him for shutting me out that I didn't spend time telling him the important things...like how much he meant to me and how much I would miss him."

"Maybe he didn't want to hear that," Gabe said, his voice soft and husky. "Maybe he couldn't have borne your sadness, and it was all he could do to control what was happening to him. Maybe he didn't want your pity and didn't want to witness your grief and your tears. And perhaps you being mad at him for shutting you out...well, maybe that made him feel *normal*...as though he wasn't defined by his illness. Like he was still the person you loved, still a healthy and strong man and not only a terminally ill cancer patient."

Lauren's throat burned. The raw truth in his words cut deep. Everything Gabe said made sense. Somehow, he knew how to reach into the depths of her soul.

She blinked to avoid the tears that threatened to spill. "Tim never got angry with me for reacting like I did. But *I* was angry with me. For a week I walked around in a daze. All I could think was how my wedding plans were ruined. I was so selfish."

"No," Gabe said gently. "Despair has many faces, Lauren. Focusing on your wedding plans was simply a coping mechanism. It's not so hard to understand."

She nodded, agreeing with him with her heart, even though her head told her to forget him and find someone who truly wanted her back. "I guess you would have seen grief like that before. I mean, dealing with patients and their families."

"I... Yes," he said quietly. "Of course."

His unwavering gaze was deeply intense and made Lauren's heart race. Heat and awareness coiled through the space between them, somehow drawing them closer, even though they were two feet apart. They weren't touching, but Lauren *felt* his presence like a lover's caress.

Suddenly, the middle road she'd been longing for seemed passionless and bland.

And the man in front of her was the one man she wanted for the rest of her life.

Chapter Nine

"Has Gabe gone home?"

Lauren picked up the tray from Cassie's bedside table and ignored the way her heart beat faster simply at the mention of his name. He'd left with the barest of goodbyes, and she'd breathed a sigh of immense relief once he'd walked out the door.

"Yes," she replied. "But he said he'd check on you in a couple of days."

"That's sweet of him," Cassie said, and grinned. "Although I'm not sure he's actually dropping by to see me."

Lauren frowned. "You're as obvious as my mother."

Her friend began ticking off his attributes on her fingers. "He's handsome, charming, single and a doctor…what more do you need?"

Commitment and love…

She wanted exactly what she'd been saying she didn't want. And neither she was likely to get from Gabe Vitali.

"He doesn't want a relationship. He's commitmentphobic." Lauren sighed heavily. "Looks, charm and medical degree aside, he's emotionally unavailable."

"I'm not so sure," Cassie said. "Maybe he's just been unlucky in love and is wary of getting close to someone again."

That's not it.

But there *was* something…some reason why he pulled back and made it clear he wanted to avoid commitment. And Lauren was sure it had nothing to do with a failed relationship. It was something else…something deeper. Something that was somehow wrapped up in the patient he lost, his decision to quit being a doctor and then choosing to move his life to Crystal Point.

"Perhaps," she said, and shrugged. "It doesn't matter anyway. He's not for me."

"Settling isn't the answer," Cassie said quietly. "I know you have this idea that you want an uncomplicated, painless relationship…but relationships *are* complicated. And they can be painful and messy. Just because things ended so tragically with Tim and then you married a man you didn't love, it doesn't mean you have to make do with ordinary."

But ordinary won't break my heart.

And Gabe would.

Hadn't he already told her as much?

"I don't believe in the fairy tale anymore," she said, and knew it was a lie. "You should rest. My folks will be home soon. I'll see you tomorrow."

She headed downstairs, and once the dishes had been done, Lauren made her way to the front living room. As always, the photographs on the mantel drew her closer. Dear Tim, she thought as she looked at his picture with a familiar sadness. Was Gabe right? Had Tim kept his illness a secret so she wouldn't pity him…so he wouldn't have to deal with her thinking of him as sick? As somehow less than a man? In the years since his death, she'd thought of his reasons countless times and always ended up believing he'd wanted to protect her from the inevitable grief and loss. But what if it was more than that? Had she been so blind? So self-centered, she hadn't considered that Tim was protecting himself, too?

When her mother arrived home, she was still sitting in the front room, still thinking about the man she'd loved and lost. And she thought about Gabe, too…and wondered how she'd managed to develop feelings for someone she hardly knew. It was different to the way she'd fallen for James. Her ex-husband hadn't made her think…want…need. He hadn't stirred her mind and body the way Gabe did. James had been an escape from the terrible anguish of losing Tim. Nothing more. She was ashamed to admit it to herself. He'd deserved better. And so had she.

By the time she returned to her house, showered and changed and rolled into bed, it was past ten. There were lights on next door, and she wondered if Gabe was up late working on the renovations in the house. Once the work was done, she was sure he'd sell the place. What then? Would they see one another as infrequently as they had before he'd moved next door?

Sleep eluded her, and after staring at the shadows bouncing off the ceiling for most of the night, Lauren snatched a few restless hours before she pulled herself out of bed at seven, dressed and drove into Bellandale. She swapped her car for the store's van and then headed back to Crystal Point Surf Club & Community Center to collect the gowns that had been left there after the benefit. She'd borrowed Cameron's key and hoped she could get the task done before Gabe arrived for work.

No such luck.

He turned up just as she was trekking the third armload of gowns down the stairs.

He stood at the bottom of the stairway. "Need some help?"

Lauren brushed past him and clutched the gowns. "No, thank you," she said as she stomped through the doorway and loaded the dresses neatly into the back of the van. When she returned inside, he was still by the stairs.

"How did you get in?" he asked.

"I borrowed my brother's keys. I didn't think it would be a big deal."

"It's not," he replied, and followed her up the stairs. "Stop being stubborn and let me help you."

Lauren glared at him. "I'm not stubborn."

He raised one dark brow. "Yeah, right," he said, and held out his arms. "Give me what needs to be taken downstairs."

Lauren's mouth tightened, but she did as he asked. It only took another twenty minutes to get everything in the van, including the three metal hanging rails he quickly pulled apart and loaded in the back of the vehicle.

"Thanks. I appreciate your help," she said as she closed the back door to the van.

"No problem. Do you want me to follow you and carry this stuff back into your store?"

"Ah, no," she said quickly. "My mother will be there to help. Thanks again."

"Do you like working with your mom?" he asked unexpectedly, and followed her around to the driver's door. "And running your own business?"

"It's what I've always done," she replied.

"Which isn't exactly an answer, is it?"

Lauren shrugged. "My mother opened the store twenty-five years ago. I took over when I graduated from business college. Do I like it?" She sighed deeply. "It's all I know. I like it well enough."

But his glittering gaze saw straight through her facade. "Sometimes it makes you unhappy."

"Some days," she admitted. "Other days it's not so bad. When I was younger, I guess I was wrapped up in the romance of it all. The gowns…the tradition… Back then it seemed to have a purpose. Now…not so much."

Because Tim died, and I discovered that not everyone gets their happy ending….

His phone beeped, and he ignored it like he had before. Lauren's eyes widened. "So did you end up calling your mother and brother?"

Gabe stared at her for a second and then grinned a little. "Not yet."

Lauren grunted under her breath. "I didn't peg you to be the inconsiderate type."

"Inconsiderate?" He repeated the word and frowned. "I'm not."

"You might want to remind your family of that the next time you speak with them," she said, and smiled ultra-sweetly. "If you ever get around to it."

Lauren watched as his resentment grew. To his credit, he kept a lid on his rising annoyance. She wasn't usually driven to lecture someone she hardly knew. He'd accused her of getting under his skin…. The problem was, he did exactly the same thing to her.

And no one had ever made her so reactive.

Gabe challenged her thoughts and ideals. He made her really *think* about things. And he had, in a matter of weeks, forced her out of the self-absorbed routine she'd disguised as her life. Even her plans to find someone to share her life with had been tainted with the memories of all she'd lost. But who was she kidding? Settling for a passionless, loveless relationship was no way to live. And in her heart, she knew she could never honor Tim by settling for less.

Looking at Gabe, it was easy to get lost in his blue eyes and handsome face…but there was so much more to him than that. And that was what she found so hard to resist. He was charming, certainly. And sexy. But he was also kind and generous, and despite her silly accusation, clearly considerate and helpful. Hadn't he come to her aid countless times? Like when she was forced to look after Jed. Or how he'd helped her dad after his fall. And he'd shown incredible concern for Cassie and her baby. There was something elementally *good* about Gabe. And that was what she was so attracted to. That was why her heart pounded whenever he was close.

That's why I've fallen in love with him....

She shivered, even though the breeze was warm.

Oh, God...it's true.

"Lauren?" His voice seemed to whisper on the wind. "Are you all right?"

She nodded, shell-shocked at the unexpected intensity of her feelings. How ironic that she'd done exactly the opposite of what she'd planned after her divorce. She'd derided attraction and desire and now found herself craving Gabe's touch more than she had ever wanted any man before. And love? She'd put it out of her head, too. Because it scared her so much to want love again.

"I'm...I'm fine," she stammered. "I have to go."

Another car pulled up just as she opened the door to the van. Two people emerged from the small yellow car. Megan and another equally pretty and sporty-looking woman in her mid-twenties. It took Lauren two seconds to notice how the other woman looked at Gabe as if she wanted to devour him.

"You could stay," he said with a grin as they approached. "For protection."

Lauren's mouth twisted. "I'm sure you're capable of protecting yourself."

"That's Megan's older sister," he explained.

"That's a woman with her eye on the prize," Lauren

said as she hopped into the van and drove off, drowning in jealousy.

And feeling like the biggest fool of all time.

It took Gabe twenty minutes to extract himself from the clutches of Megan's persistent sibling. She reminded him that her name was Cara and asked for his number. He avoided answering her, pleading a pile of urgent paperwork on his desk.

Once she left and Megan headed to the beach for her patrol shift, Gabe wrote a list of things he needed to do for the day.

Thing number one: stop thinking about Lauren.
Thing number two: stop dreaming about Lauren.

He snatched a glance at his cell phone on the desk. He really should call his mother. And Aaron. But he just wasn't in the mood to talk. Or to be talked *at*. His mom would know something was up. She'd dig and dig until he admitted that he'd met someone. That he *liked* someone. And that his beautiful next-door neighbor was driving him crazy.

Then Claire Vitali would want to know everything.

And he had nothing to say.

Lauren was broken emotionally. He was broken physically. It could never work. The more he knew her, the more it served to strengthen his resolve. Even though he could have easily talked himself into it. The way she looked at him, the way she'd responded to his kiss at the benefit, the way she argued and contradicted him at every opportunity… It was like pouring gasoline on a bonfire. Everything about Lauren drew him in. Her face, her body, the sweet floral scent of her skin…every part of her connected with every part of him.

Which was as inconvenient as hell.

Even more inconvenient was the sight of Megan's sister standing on his doorstep at seven o'clock that evening. He'd been home for several hours. He'd changed and gone for a run, then returned home to work on painting one of the guest rooms. He'd just emerged from showering and pulling on fresh jeans and a T-shirt when the tall brunette had arrived on his doorstep clutching the textbook he'd loaned to Megan. Returning the book had been her excuse for dropping by, and he made a mental note to query Megan about handing out his address.

His visitor managed to wheedle her way up the hall and into the front living room, and Gabe was just about all out of patience when he heard another knock on his front door. Gabe told Cara to stay put and headed up the hallway.

Lauren stood beneath the porch light. In a long floral skirt and pale blue T-shirt she almost stole his breath. Gabe quickly pulled himself together.

"Hey...what's up?" he asked.

She held out an envelope. "The estimate for the fence looks reasonable. There's a check in there with my half of the initial payment."

"Thanks for getting back to me," he said quietly and took the note. "I'll let the contractor know he can start as soon as possible."

She shrugged, and the T-shirt slipped off her shoulder a little. "Okay."

The sight of her bare skin heated his blood, and he swallowed hard. "If you like, I'll—"

"Gabe?"

Great.

His unwelcome guest chose that moment to come sauntering down the hall, hips swaying, calling his name. He saw Lauren's expression tighten. And as stupid as he knew it was, he didn't want her thinking he was entertaining some random woman in his home.

"Sorry," she said, breathing harder than usual. "I didn't realize you had company."

"I don't," he said, and her brows shot up instantly. It was stupid. They weren't together. They weren't dating. They weren't sleeping together.

One kiss...that was all it was...

And even though there was nothing going on with the unwanted woman in his hallway, Gabe still felt like an unfaithful jerk.

"You can do what you like," Lauren shot back, and swiveled on her heels.

She quickly disappeared down the garden, and Gabe let out an impatient sigh.

"You have to go," he said to the woman now at his side. "Good night."

Minutes later, after quickly packing Cara into her car and waving her off, Gabe walked around the hedge and tapped on Lauren's door. The screen was locked, but the door was open, and he could hear her banging pots in the kitchen.

He called her name. She responded with more banging. She was mad. And she was jealous. The notion made him grin stupidly.

"Lauren, come out here and talk to me."

"Go away."

"Not until you let me explain."

"I don't want to hear it," she said, and banged some more.

Gabe expelled a heavy breath and leaned against the door. "She was just returning a book I loaned to—"

"Yeah, I'm sure it's her reading skills that you like," she said loudly, cutting him off.

"I don't like anything about her," he said, and sighed. "I hardly know her. She was returning a book I loaned to her sister. Now, will you come to the door so we can stop yelling?"

Pots banged again. "I said, go away."

Exasperated, Gabe straightened his back. "I hardly know her, like I said. You've no reason to be jealous."

The banging stopped. Gabe waited, but she didn't come to the door. The sudden silence was almost eerie. After a few minutes, he gave up and headed down the steps. He'd been back in his own house for about ten minutes when he heard the sharp rap on his front door. Lauren stood on the other side of the screen, cheeks ablaze, chest heaving.

He pushed the screen back and watched, fascinated and suddenly wholly aroused as she glared at him, hands planted on her hips.

"I. Am. Not. Jealous."

Oh, yeah, she was.

Gabe raised a brow. "No?"

Lauren pulled the screen out of his grasp and held it back farther. "No."

"I think you are."

"And I think you're an egotistical jerk," she shot back. "I've no interest in anything you do."

Every feeling, every ounce of desire he had for her rose up, and in that moment, Gabe was powerless to do anything other than smile broadly. "Then why are you on my doorstep?"

Lauren's resolve crumbled a little. Damn him. She shouldn't have let her temper get the better of her. Coming to his door was crazy thinking. "Because…we're arguing and I—"

"No, we're not," he said, and reached out to take her hand. "I think…" He paused, looking deep into her eyes. "I think this is more like foreplay than an argument."

Lauren flushed and pulled back. "Of all the conceited—"

"Let's not have this discussion on the doorstep, okay?" he said as he turned and walked down the hall.

Lauren stayed where she was for a moment. *I should turn around and go home.*

I really should.

Instead, she crossed the threshold, closed the door and followed him into the living room. When she entered the room, she saw he was standing by the sofa. And he was smiling. Lauren wasn't sure if she wanted to slug him or kiss him.

"Come here," he said softly.

She took a deep breath and stepped toward him. "You are the most—"

"That woman who was here earlier is Megan's sister, Cara. She returned a book I loaned to Megan," he said, cutting her off again. "Megan is sitting a nurse's entrance exam next week," he said quietly, cutting her off again. "And that's all. She may have had another motive, but I'm *not* interested in her...okay?"

Her heart raced.

Oh, sweet heaven. She tried to ignore the heat that traveled across her skin as well as the seductive sound of his voice. But failed. Every sense she possessed was on high alert.

"I shouldn't care what you do..." When he grasped her hand, she crumbled some more. "Gabe...I...I just..."

He lightly shrugged his magnificent shoulders and gently urged her closer until there was barely a whisper of space between them. "I can't fight this anymore," he admitted hoarsely. "I want to. I know I need to, for your sake, because you deserve more than the empty words of a future I simply can't promise you. And I've really tried to stop wanting you...but I can't."

There was such raw passion in his words, and Lauren's breath was sucked from her lungs. She moved closer and they touched, chest against breast. Gabe wound his arms around her, urging her against him.

"I've tried, too," she said through a sigh.

Gabe touched her face and kept his gaze connected with hers as he rubbed his thumb gently across her chin. Lauren tilted her head back and smiled. In all her life, she'd never experienced anything like the sensation of being near Gabe, or his soft, mesmerizing touch.

Their mouths met, and Lauren's head spun. His kiss was like nothing on earth. His hands were warm against her back, his mouth gentle as he coaxed a response. Lauren gave it willingly. She would give him anything. Everything. And the revelation rocked her through to the core.

I am so in love with him. Completely, irrevocably, crazily.

She opened her mouth, tasted his tongue against her own, felt a rush of pleasure coil up her spine and across her skin. She whispered his name against his lips, and Gabe urged her closer. Lauren sighed deeply from that way-down place, which was fueled by need and longing and a powerful rush of desire.

"I want to make love to you," he whispered raggedly, moving his mouth from her lips to her cheek. "So much."

Lauren moaned, all resistance gone. *Just for tonight. I can have this. I can have him. I can pretend it will work out.* "I want that, too."

Gabe grasped her hand and led her down the hall and into his bedroom. He released her and flicked on the bedside lamp. The big bed was covered in a patterned blue quilt, and she swallowed hard as nerves spectacularly set in. His gaze never left her, and she felt the heat of his gaze through to her bones.

"So…here we are."

Lauren didn't move. "Here we are." She managed a tiny smile. "I'm a little nervous."

"You don't need to be."

There was desire and passion and tenderness in his eyes. He wouldn't rush her. He wouldn't coerce or manipulate her with empty words. He opened the bedside drawer, found a condom and dropped the packet on the mattress, and even that made her long for him all the more. He was sweet and considerate. He was everything she wanted.

"Lauren, come here."

She moved toward him and stopped about a foot away. Desire and heat swept through the room with seductive force. She wished she'd had a chance to change into something sexy and filmy. The skirt and T-shirt seemed way too ordinary.

She rested her hands against his chest and then trailed down to the hem of his shirt. "Take this off," she said boldly, and saw him smile.

Gabe pulled the shirt over his head and dropped it on the floor. "Better?"

Lauren nodded. "Much," she replied, and traced her fingertips down the middle of his bare chest and twirled her fingers through the dark hair. She noticed a faded crisscross of small scars near the curve of his armpit and instinctively reached up to outline a finger along the skin there.

He tensed instantly.

"What's this from?" she asked softly.

"It's…nothing," he replied, equally as quiet. "Forget about it."

"Gabe, I—"

"Shh," he said, and placed two fingers gently against her lips. "Later. Right now, let's forget about the past. Let's be in *this* moment."

Lauren's eyes widened as she slid out of her sandals. She liked the sound of that. She dropped her hands and deliberately took her time as she gripped the edge of the T-shirt and slowly lifted it up and over her shoulders. Then she tossed it onto the foot of the bed and inhaled deeply. The white lace bra she wore was modest, but beneath the smoldering brilliance of Gabe's blue eyes, she felt as though it was the sexiest piece of underwear on the entire planet.

Heat charged between them, and she pushed past any lingering insecurity. He wanted her. That kind of look couldn't be faked. He had no agenda. She sucked in a breath and spoke. "Your turn."

He quickly flipped off his shoes and grinned in such a sexy way, her legs trembled. "Back to you."

She sucked in more air, willed strength into her knees as she unzipped her skirt and hooked her thumbs into the waistband. She heard his breath catch, saw the hot desire in his eyes. And waited. Took a breath. Then met his gaze head-on and slowly stripped the garment over her hips. She pushed it aside with her foot and rounded out her shoulders. Her briefs were white cotton and lace high-cuts. Not nearly seductive enough. Not the kind that aroused desire. Except Gabe looked hotly aroused, and it made her want him all the more.

"So," Lauren said, way more steadily than she felt. "You?"

Gabe's hands stilled on his belt, and his smile was pure sexual heat. He released the buckle and slid the belt from the loops. "Done," he said, and dropped it on the carpet. "Next?"

At a distinct disadvantage, Lauren smiled and backed up toward the bed. She reached around and slowly unclipped her bra, then eased herself from the shoulder straps and pulled the garment free. The bra fell from her fingertips and landed at her feet.

He looked at her and let out a ragged groan. Her nipples peaked instantly. "Okay...enough."

Lauren wondered what he meant for a microsecond, wondered if he found her lacking. But then he was in front of her, reaching for her, wrapping his arms around her. His mouth hovered over her eager lips, waiting to claim, waiting for her surrender. She gave it, completely and wholly and pressed against his chest. He captured her mouth in a searing kiss and gently fisted a handful of her hair. There was no force, no reticence, only need and desire and the realization it was the perfect kiss. The perfect moment. And all other kisses were quickly forgotten.

They tumbled onto the bed, mouths still together, hands moving over skin. He cupped one breast, and Lauren moaned low in the throat. His fingers were firm yet gentle, his mouth hot against her as he trailed down her cheeks, to her neck and then lower still, to where she ached for his touch. There was magic in his hands and mouth, and Lauren experienced a surge of feeling so intense, so deep, that it warmed her through to her bones. For the first time in forever, she was exactly where she wanted to be, and she sighed heavily as she shook in his arms.

"What is it?" Gabe asked and looked up. "Are you okay?"

Lauren smiled and touched his face. "I'm fine. Don't stop," she pleaded, and grabbed his shoulders.

"I have no intention of stopping," he said, and kissed her hungrily.

It was what she wanted to hear. What she needed to hear. The kissing went on, soft and hard, slow and fast, mesmerizing and wholly arousing. Lauren pushed against him, felt the abrasive denim rub across her thighs. "You're still wearing too many clothes," she whispered, and placed a hand on the band of his jeans.

He smiled against her skin. "You, too," he said, and pushed her briefs over her hips in one smooth movement. The way Gabe looked at her was real and heady and made her spin.

Naked and without inhibitions, Lauren curved against

him and popped the top button on his jeans. She tugged at the zipper and laughed delightfully when he rolled her over and kissed her again.

"Please," she begged softly, and grabbed the waistband again.

"Relax, Lauren," he said, and curved a hand down her back and over her hip. "There's no need to hurry."

He was wrong. There was a need to hurry. She wanted him desperately. She wanted to feel his skin against her, taste his kiss over and over and have the weight of his strong body above her, inside her. It was a need unlike any Lauren had ever known. "I want you," she said against his mouth. "Now."

"Soon," he promised, and moved his hand between them, stroking her where she longed to be touched with skillful, gentle intimacy. Tremors fluttered across her skin, and Lauren responded instantly. The heat grew as her breath quickened, and she let herself go, up and up, shaken by a white-hot, incandescent pleasure so intense, she could barely draw breath. She'd forgotten that feeling—forgotten how good it felt to experience such powerful release. Gabe kissed her again and smothered her soft groans and whispered pleas.

She laid her hands on his jeans and felt him hard against the denim. "You really are wearing too many clothes."

He nodded and swung his legs off the mattress. As he watched her, the connection between them shimmered. Then he smiled that lovely smile she longed for more than any other. Seconds later, his remaining clothes were off, and once the condom was in place, he was beside her on the big bed. They kissed again, long, hot kisses, tongues dancing together, skin on skin. She touched him as she'd wanted to do for weeks—his thighs, his arms, his back. His smooth skin burned beneath her fingertips, and when his mouth found her breast and he gently toyed with the nipple, she arched her spine off the bed. He moved above her and Lauren lay back, urging him closer. She wrapped her arms around his strong shoulders, opened herself for him and waited for that moment. He rested on his elbows, hovered above her and looked into her face with scorching intimacy.

The moment was achingly sweet and unbelievably erotic at the same time.

He nudged against her until finally they were together. Lauren sighed deep in her throat. She loved the feel of him. Being with Gabe felt right. He didn't move for a moment, didn't do anything other than stare deeply into her eyes.

"You're so beautiful, you take my breath away," he said softly.

It was a lovely, romantic notion, and Lauren absorbed his words right though to her heart. No one had ever spoken to her with such quiet tenderness. She blinked back tears and shuddered, feeling every part of him against her in a way she'd never experienced before.

He moved, and she went with him, up and over into that place where only they existed.

Chapter Ten

Gabe stirred, stretched out and took a deep breath. The soft scent of flowers played around in his memory. Lauren. He snaked an arm across the sheets, expecting to find her asleep beside him. But he was alone.

The digital clock on the bedside table read 4:00 a.m. A thin sliver of streetlight shone through a gap in the curtains, and he heard a dog barking in the distance.

Gabe swung off the bed, grabbed his briefs and jeans from the floor and pulled them on. He left the bedroom, padded down the hall and found Lauren in the kitchen, sitting at the table with a mug between her hands. Her tousled hair and T-shirt was enough to stir his blood. He could easily make love to her again. And again. And every day for the rest of his life.

Whoa.

He couldn't promise that. What if he didn't have a rest of his life? Only now. This moment. If his illness returned, he wasn't about to drag Lauren into what that would mean.

She'd been through enough. She already buried the one man she'd loved. How could he do that to her again?

She looked up when he entered the room and smiled. "Hi. Tea?" she offered, and tapped the mug.

"Sure," Gabe said, even though he didn't really care for the stuff. He watched her get up, move around the counter and flick on the kettle. "Couldn't sleep?" he asked.

She shook her head and grabbed a mug from the cupboard. "Not really. Sorry if I woke you."

Gabe walked into the galley. "Everything all right?"

"Sure," she said quietly, and popped a tea bag into the mug. "I'm not a sound sleeper. Comes from living alone, I guess."

"You're not alone now, though."

The kettle dinged, and she poured the water. "For the moment...no."

An odd twitch caught him behind the ribs. He stepped closer and touched her arm. "Lauren, forget the tea."

She inhaled and turned toward him. "You mean you want to have *the* talk? Before you skedaddle me back home?"

There was a familiar spark in her eyes, and it was a look he knew. She was annoyed with him. "I mean, forget the tea and come back to bed."

She twisted back to the sink. "I thought we'd have—"

"A postmortem?" He reached across and touched her cheek. Unable to help himself, he smiled. "Let's not do that. You think too much."

"I don't," she insisted. "And it's insensitive of you to laugh at me."

Gabe gathered her in his arms, kissed her forehead and spoke gently. "You're being a little ridiculous, you know that?"

She sagged against his chest, and he tightened his grip. "I know. I'm just not used to feeling like this. I'm not used to *doing* this. We hardly know one another. I was looking for something else, and then you move in next door with your blue eyes and nice smile and I was...I was..."

He pulled back and softly grasped her chin. "You were what?"

She let out a long breath. "Done for."

Gabe's insides contracted. What was she saying? That it was more than a developing friendship and blinding physical attraction? That she loved him?

Sure, he had feelings for Lauren. A lot of feelings. And making love with her had been out of this world. But falling in love wasn't part of his plan. Hell, it was out of the question at the moment. Not when he didn't know if he actually *had* a future. He had a five-year plan and intended to stick to it. Lauren deserved more than empty promises. Or another casket to grieve over.

"Lauren, we're friends and I'd—"

"Friends with benefits?" she said, and cut him off as she pulled away. "I really hate that expression. It's a convenient line to avoid commitment."

Gabe bit back a frustrated sigh. "The only thing I'm trying to avoid is hurting you."

She blinked hard. "Well, you're not doing so great."

He knew that. There were tears in her eyes, and he'd put them there. "If I'd thought you wouldn't be—"

"Forget the condescending speech, Gabe," she said, cutting him off again. "I'm sorry I'm not able to take the emotion out of sex. Blame it on my traditional upbringing, but I've always thought that making love should mean exactly that."

She was right. It should. "I agree. And there was nothing casual about last night for me, Lauren. But I can't promise you more than this...." He paused and took a breath. "More than now. I can't say what the future will bring, and I don't know where I'll be."

She pulled herself from his embrace. "Are you leaving? Going somewhere? Are you going back to California? Is that why you—"

"No," he said quickly, and urged her close again. "Of course not."

"Then what do you mean?"

Guilt hit him between the shoulder blades. *Tell her the truth....*

But he couldn't. "Forget it. Come back to bed, Lauren."

Her eyes glistened, and she nodded.

Back in his bedroom they made love again. This time it was quicker, hotter, as though they had a need that had to be sated. Afterward, Lauren stretched and sighed and curved against him. And he was, Gabe realized as he drifted back to sleep, happier and more content than he could ever remember being before in his life.

At seven, Lauren rolled out of bed and met Gabe in the kitchen, wearing only a navy blue bathrobe he'd offered. He'd made pancakes, and she'd agreed to try them before she returned home to shower and change and head to the store. Despite her earlier display of emotion, there was an easy companionship between them, as if they'd done it before, as if they knew one another deeply and intimately.

Which they did, she figured, coloring a little when she remembered the way they'd made love just hours ago. Being with Gabe was like nothing she'd experienced before. He was an incredibly generous lover. He was thoughtful and attentive, and they were well matched in bed.

What about out of bed?

Was there enough between them to stand up to the test outside the bedroom? She hoped so. He'd made no promises, offered no suggestions that their relationship would go beyond one night together. But there was no doubt in her mind that what they'd shared was more than simply sex.

"Are you okay?" he asked, watching her as she mulled over her second mug of tea.

Lauren looked up and smiled. "Fine. Just thinking I should get moving. I have to open the store this morning, and if I'm late, my mother will ask a thousand questions."

He grinned. "Can I see you tonight?"

Lauren's insides jumped. "Are you asking me out on a date?"

"Yes."

Her brows arched. "That's quite a commitment. You sure you're ready for that?"

He came around the table and gently pulled her to her feet. "I guess we'll find out as we go."

He kissed her with a fierce intensity that had *possession* stamped all over it. And Lauren didn't mind one bit. They made out for a few minutes, and when he released her, Lauren was left breathless and wanting him all the more.

"I'll just grab the rest of my clothes," she said with a smile as she left the kitchen.

Back in his bedroom, she gathered up her clothes and quickly changed back into her underwear, skirt and T-shirt. She found her shoes at the foot of the bed and slipped into them before she walked into the en-suite bathroom to return the robe. She hung it on a hook and turned toward the mirror. Only to be faced with her pale complexion and mussed *bed* hair.

She moaned and finger combed her bangs. There were remnants of mascara clinging to her lashes, and she looked for a tissue to wipe beneath her eyes. When she found nothing on the counter, Lauren opened the overhead cabinet. And stilled immediately.

A long row of medication bottles caught her attention. Serious medication. Very serious. She'd seen similar medication bottles before. Along the same shelf, there were vitamins and several homeopathic tonics. Lauren's blood ran cold. Why would a strong, healthy man like Gabe need so much medicine? It didn't make sense. She suppressed the urge to examine one of the bottles, but her mind continued to race. A rush of possibilities scrambled in her head. He was a doctor...perhaps it was something to do with that?

It's none of my business.

But she still longed to know.

Immediately embarrassed that she'd even noticed the bottles, she was about to shut the cabinet when she heard a sound from the doorway.

"Lauren?"

Gabe's voice. Marred with concern and query. She turned to face him and found his expression was completely closed off. Unreadable. Guarded.

Her mouth turned dry. "I was...I was looking for a tissue." She stopped speaking and looked at him. "I'm sorry, I shouldn't have opened the—"

He stepped forward and closed the cabinet door. "You should leave if you're going to open your store on time," he said flatly.

Lauren's stomach lurched. He looked solemn. He looked annoyed; he looked as though she'd invaded his privacy in the worst possible way.

"What's going on, Gabe?" she asked, stepping out of the en suite and into the bedroom. "Why are you—"

"I'll see you out," he said, and swiveled on his heels.

Lauren followed him out of the room and was halfway down the hallway when she said his name. He stopped and turned.

"What?" he asked.

"Exactly," she said. *"What?"*

They were now both in the living room doorway, neither moving. He was tense, on edge, and Lauren resisted the urge to reach out and touch him. He looked as if he wanted her gone. And the notion hurt through to her bones.

"It's nothing," he said quietly. "We should both get ready for work."

Lauren shook her head. "Don't do that. Don't shut me out."

Silence stretched between them like a piece of worn, brittle elastic. Somehow, the incredible night making love with one another and the lovely relaxed morning sharing pancakes and kisses had morphed into a defining, uncomfortable moment in the hallway.

All because she'd seen medication in a bathroom cabinet.

An odd feeling silently wound its way through her blood and across her skin. And a tiny voice whispered in the back of her mind. As the seconds ticked, the whispering became louder, more insistent. Something was wrong. Had she missed signals? Had she been so wrapped up in herself she hadn't really seen him? And without knowing how or why, Lauren suspected the answer was within her grasp.

Just ask the question.... Ask him.... Ask him, and he'll tell you....

"Gabe…" Her voice trailed off for a few moments and she quickly regathered her thoughts. "Are you…sick?"

Shutters came down over his face. She'd seen the look before—that day at the hospital when they'd met near the elevator. He'd been coming from the direction of the specialist offices. *The oncology specialist.* Lauren scrambled her thoughts together. Suddenly, she wasn't sure she wanted to hear his reply.

"No," he said finally.

"But…"

"I was," he said when her query faded. "Eighteen months ago."

A sharp pain tightened her chest. A terrible, familiar pain that quickly took hold of her entire body. It was hard to breathe, and she didn't want to hear any more. But she pressed on.

"What did you—"

"Hodgkin's lymphoma," he said impassively, cutting her off.

Cancer...

Lauren's knees weakened. He'd had cancer.

Just like Tim.

She swallowed the thick emotion in her throat. Every memory, every fear, every feeling of despair and pain she'd experienced with Tim rose up and consumed her like a wave. Tears burned the backs of her eyes, and she struggled to keep them at bay as a dozen questions buzzed on her tongue.

And then, like a jigsaw in her mind, the scattered pieces of the puzzle came together.

Gabe seemed to understand the despair she'd experienced at losing Tim. And he also seemed to understand the other man's motives better than she ever had. Gabe didn't want commitment. He wasn't interested in a relationship.

If you waste your heart on me, I'll break it....

She put her hand to her mouth and shuddered. It was too much. Too hard. Too familiar. And then she ran. Out of his bedroom. Out of his house. Out of his life.

By midday, Gabe was silently thanking Lauren for doing what he couldn't. For walking away.

For racing away...

It was better than facing what he'd expected—the reflection, the realization. *The pity.*

Of course she'd taken off. What sane, sensible woman wouldn't? It certainly hadn't taken Mona long to find the door once he'd given his ex-girlfriend an opportunity to bail on their relationship. She hadn't wanted to waste her life on a man with a death sentence.

And neither would Lauren.

Which is what he wanted, right? No involvement, no feelings, no risk.

Now he just had to convince himself.

Last night had been incredible. The best sex he'd ever had. But it had been a mistake. And wholly unfair to Lauren. From the beginning, she'd been clear on what she wanted, and Gabe knew he'd somehow ambushed that goal by allowing himself to get involved with her. He had a five-year plan, and he still intended sticking to it.

He got a text message from Aaron around two o'clock.

You still haven't called Mom.

He replied after a few minutes and got back to work.

I'll get to it.

When?

Gabe snatched the phone up and responded.

When I do. Back off.

He turned the cell to mute, logged off the computer and sat deep in his chair. He was, he realized as he stared at the blank screen, out-of-his-mind bored with his job. Shuffling paperwork during the week and attending to jellyfish stings and sunstroke on the weekends simply didn't cut it. He wanted more. He needed more.

During the night, in between making love with Lauren and holding her in his arms, they'd talked about his career. For the first time since he'd left Huntington Beach, Gabe admitted how much he missed practicing medicine. As he

sat at the desk that had never felt like his own, Gabe knew
what he had to do.

It was after four, and he was just finishing a promis-
ing call with the human resources director at Bellandale's
hospital when there was a tap on the door. It was Lauren.

She entered the room and closed the door.

"Hi," she said quietly. "Can we talk?"

Gabe's stomach tightened. She looked so lovely in her
sensible black skirt and green blouse. She'd come to end
it. Terrific. It was exactly what he expected. *And* what he
wanted. They'd stay friends and neighbors and that was all.
Perhaps *friends* was stretching it, too. A clean break—that
was what they needed.

He nodded. "Sure."

Her hands were clasped tightly together. "I wanted to…
I'd like to…"

Gabe stood and moved around the desk. "You'd like to
what?"

She sighed and then took a long, unsteady breath. "To
apologize. I shouldn't have left the way I did this morning.
I think I was so…so…overwhelmed by it all, by what you
told me…I just reacted. And badly. Forgive me?"

Gabe shrugged. "There's nothing to forgive. Your reaction was perfectly normal."

"Don't do that," she said, and frowned. "Don't make it
okay. It's not okay."

"I can't tell you how to feel. Or how to respond to
things." He perched his behind on the desk. "Considering
what you've been through in the past, it makes sense that
you'd react as you did."

"It's because of what I've been through in the past that
I should *not* have reacted that way. I'm ashamed that I ran
out this morning without asking you anything about it. But
I'm here now. And I'd like to know." Her concerned expression spoke volumes. Gabe knew that look. He knew

what was coming. He waited for it. "Would you tell me about your illness?"

And there it was.

Pity...

His illness. As though it suddenly defined him. As though that was all he was. The ultimate unequalizer. Healthy people to one side. Sick people to the other.

Gabe took a breath. Best he get it over with. "There's not much to tell. I was diagnosed with lymphoma. I had surgery and treatment. And I still take some medication. End of story."

She nodded, absorbing his words. "And you're okay now?"

"Maybe."

She frowned. "What does that mean?"

"It means there are no guarantees. It means that my last round of tests came back clear. It means that without a re-currence within five years, I should be fine."

Should be. Could be. Maybe.

If she had any sense, she'd turn around and run again.

"And that's why you don't want a serious relationship?" she asked, not running.

Gabe met her gaze. At that moment, he didn't know what the hell he wanted other than to drag her into his arms and kiss her as if there was no tomorrow. But he wouldn't. "Exactly."

"Because you might get sick again?" Her hands twisted self-consciously. "Isn't that a little...pessimistic?"

"Realistic," he corrected.

She stepped a little closer. "Then why did you make love to me last night?"

Because I'm crazy about you. Because when I'm near you, I can't think straight.

"I'm attracted to you," he said quietly.

"And that's all?"

"It's all I can offer," he said, and saw her eyes shadow. He didn't want to hurt her, but he wasn't about to make any grand statements, either. She'd be better off forgetting him and resuming her search for Mr. Middle-of-the-Road. "You know what you want and that's not…me. I care about you, Lauren, too much to lead you on."

Her eyes widened, and she laughed shrilly. "You're joking, right?"

"No."

"That's a convenient line for a man who's *afraid* of commitment."

Gabe squashed the annoyance snaking up his spine. "I'm not afraid of—"

"Sure you are," she shot back quickly, and waved her arms. "You work here instead of the job you're trained to do, even though you're clearly a skilled doctor. You won't even commit to a phone call to your family. And let's not forget the meaningless one-night stands."

"That's an interesting judgment from someone who can't bear to be alone."

As soon as he said the words, Gabe knew he'd pushed a button. But damn, couldn't she see that he wanted to make it easier for her, not harder?

Her eyes flashed molten fire. "I *can* be alone. But I'd prefer to not be. And maybe you think that makes me weak and needy." She cocked a brow. "And you know what—perhaps it does. But I'd rather be like that than be too scared to try."

Gabe's gut lurched. He didn't want to admit anything. She was right when she said he was scared. But he couldn't tell her that. Because she'd want to know why. "You don't know what you're asking."

She shook her head fractionally. "I'm not asking anything. I never have. I like you, Gabe. I…I more than *like* you. I wouldn't have spent last night with you if I didn't feel—"

"You want a future, Lauren," he said, and cut her off before she said something she'd inevitably regret. "A future that includes marriage and children and a lifetime together." He inhaled deeply. "It's a future we all take for granted. Until you're told you might not have it."

"But you said you were okay now."

"The cancer could still come back. I wasn't given a one hundred percent chance of making it past five years," he said, and ran a hand through his hair. "Not exactly dead man walking, but close enough that I knew I had to make a few decisions."

Her mouth thinned. "Decisions?"

"About my life," he explained. "About how I wanted to *live* my life. I left my home, my career and my family because I'd had enough of people treating me as though I was somehow changed…or that having cancer had changed me. Because despite how much I didn't want to admit it, I was changed. I am changed. And until I know for sure that I have a future, I'm not going to jump into a relationship." He stared at her. "Not with anyone."

"Jump?" She shook her head. "Most of the time I feel as though you've been dragged into this by your ankles. So, I guess *jumping* into bed with me doesn't count?"

"Of course it counts, and that's exactly my point," he replied. "But I can't give you what you want. I can't and won't make that kind of promise. It wouldn't be fair to you, Lauren. I've had eighteen months to think about this, and I didn't come to the decision lightly. I'm not going to get involved here, only to…"

"To what?"

He sucked in a breath. "To die."

Lauren stepped back and wrapped her arms tightly

around herself. He knew she heard fear in his voice, and he hated the sympathy in her eyes. But she kept on, relentless.

"I don't need that kind of promise, Gabe."

He shook his head. "You do. You would. If we got serious, you'd want it. Hell, you'd deserve it. And I couldn't give it to you."

"How do you know?" she asked. "You're imagining the worst when—"

He made a frustrated sound. "Because I just know. Because I've lived with it for eighteen months. I know what being sick did to the people around me. As a doctor, I saw sickness every day and didn't have one clue what my patients went through until I found myself on the other side of the hospital bed."

"I wasn't one of those people."

"No, you weren't. But you know how this could work out." He raised a hand dismissively. "You've been through it, you grieved…you're *still* grieving for Tim and that life you'd planned for."

"This isn't about Tim," she said quickly. "This is about you. Tim had a terminal illness. An inoperable brain tumor. He was dying…you're not."

"I might," he said flatly.

"So could I. No one can expect that kind of guarantee."

"Isn't that why you married a man you didn't love?" he asked. "Because he was healthy and could give you that kind of assurance?"

"I was—"

"You were looking for your happily ever after," he said, frustrated and annoyed and aching inside. "You were looking for a man who could give you the life you'd dreamed about. I can't do that. Damn it, I don't even know if I could give you the children you want so badly."

Her face crumbled. "Oh, I hadn't thought about—"

"About the possible side effects of chemotherapy and radiation." Gabe expelled a heavy breath. "Well, think about this…there are *no* guarantees. And as much as you say you don't want them, we both know you do. Go home, Lauren," he said coldly, knowing he was hurting her, and knowing he had to. "Go home and forget about this."

Forget about me.

Seconds later, she was gone.

Chapter Eleven

Lauren left the store early on Thursday afternoon and arrived home to find two battered trucks in Gabe's driveway and one in hers. The fence between the two properties, which had long since been hidden by the overgrown hedge, was now in piles of broken timber on both front lawns. She maneuvered her small vehicle around the truck and parked under the carport.

One of the workers came around to her car and apologized up front for the noise they were making and said they'd be finished for the day within a couple of hours.

"But that tree has got to go," he said, grinning toothlessly.

The tree was a tall pine that sat on the fence line and often dropped its branches on her roof. It wasn't much of a tree, and her brother had offered several times to remove it for her.

"Oh, really?"

"The root system will wreck the new fence. We'll get started on it this afternoon, if that's okay?"

Lauren shrugged. "No problem."

Once inside, she changed into jeans and white T-shirt and set her laptop up on the kitchen table. She had invoicing and wages to do and preferred to do it without the inevitable distractions at the store. She poured a glass of iced tea and sat down to work.

By four-thirty, the contractors were still at it. And they were noisy. They were digging new post holes along the fence line with a machine that made a loud *clunk* sound with every rotation. And the buzz of dueling chainsaws didn't help her concentration.

Not that she was in a concentrating mood. For two days, she'd been walking around on autopilot, working at the store, talking to her mother, pretending nothing was wrong when she was broken inside.

Gabe's words still haunted her. His admittance that he might not be able to father children played over and over in her mind. In her heart, she knew that didn't matter to her. Sure, she wanted children. She longed for them. But she wanted Gabe more. Even though he didn't want her back.

At the store that day, she'd arrived early and took inventory on a range of new arrivals. When that was done, she'd dressed two of the windows with new gowns and played around with matching accessories. When she was finished, she'd stood back and examined the results. Not bad, she'd thought. How long had it been since she'd enjoyed her work? *Years.* Too long. After Tim died, she'd lost interest in the fashions and could barely tolerate the enthusiasm of the clients looking for their perfect gown. Her own fairy tale was over, and Lauren took little pleasure in anything related to weddings or the store. It had stopped being fun and instead became a duty.

Perhaps it was time to sell the business and try something new?

She'd once had dreams of taking a break from the store when she was married and had a family of her own. But Tim's death had changed everything, and now that dream seemed as unreachable as the stars around some distant planet. Because despite how much she'd convinced herself it was what she wanted, her plans for a loveless, passionless relationship were stupid. If falling for Gabe had shown her nothing else, Lauren now knew what she wanted. Along with friendship and compatibility, love and passion were vital. In fact, she wanted it all. Everything. A full and complete relationship.

Maybe a vacation was in order. She hadn't been on a holiday for years. Perhaps that would quell her discontented spirit. In the meantime, she'd talk with her mother about putting on another part-time employee so she could take some time off. She thought she might even go back to college.

And she'd get over Gabe. She had to.

Lauren was just about to get herself a second glass of iced tea when she heard an almighty bang, followed by several loud shouts and then a crash and the booming sound of timber cracking. Another sound quickly followed—this one a hollow rumble that chilled her to the bone. The roof above creaked and groaned, and suddenly parts of the ceiling gave way as tiles and branches came cascading through the gaping hole now in her roof. She dived under the table as prickly branches and sharp barbs of shattered timber fell through the gap. Plaster from the ceiling showered across the room in a haze of dust and debris, and she coughed hard as it shot up her nose and into her lungs.

When it was over, she heard more shouts and the sound of heavy boot steps on the roof. She coughed again and wiped her watery eyes. Still crouching, she shuffled backward but quickly moved back when she felt a sharp sting on her left arm. A jagged branch had sliced her skin, and she clamped her right hand across the wound to stem the flow of blood. When that didn't help she noticed her T-shirt was ripped in several places, so Lauren quickly tore off a strip from the hem and made a makeshift bandage to wrap around her arm.

She moved forward and tried to make another exit point, but the branches were thick and too heavy for her to maneuver out of the way. Lauren swallowed the dust in her throat and coughed again. The kitchen table was completely covered in branches and debris from the ceiling support beams, shattered roof tiles and plaster. Her legs started to stiffen in their crouched position, and she stretched forward, looking for a way out from under the table. She tried to push a few of the smaller branches out of the way, but the sharp ends pinched her hands.

She could have been badly injured. Or worse. But she quickly put that thought from her mind and decided to wait for workers to come and help her. And finally, she heard a voice and heaved a relieved sigh.

"Lauren!"

Gabe. Her heart thundered in her chest when she heard footsteps down the hallway and then the sound of tiles crunching beneath his feet. She could see his jeans-clad legs through the twisted branches.

"Where are you?" he asked urgently, coming closer.

"I'm under here," she said, and rattled one of the branches. "Under the table."

"Are you hurt?"

"A few scratches," she replied, coughing again and ignoring the throbbing sting from the gash on her arm. "But I think I'm mostly okay. I have a cut on my arm."

"Stay still, and I'll be there as quickly as I can."

He immediately made his way through the room, easily hauling fallen plaster and timber out of his path. The branches around the table shook and swayed, and she heard him curse under his breath. Within seconds, he'd made a space large enough for her to crawl through. He crouched down, and relief coursed through her veins. She pushed back the swell of emotion rising up.

"Give me your hand," he said, and she reached out.

His fingers clasped around hers, warm and strong and lovely and safe. Lauren stifled a sob as he gently drew her out through the space and got her to her feet. And without a word, he folded her into his arms and held her close.

"I've got you," he whispered into her hair as he gently stroked her scalp. "You're okay now."

Relief pitched behind her ribs, and as Lauren glanced around, the enormity of the destruction struck her like a lash. The room was wrecked. Plaster and timber were strewn over the floor, and benches and dust from the shattered ceiling plaster covered every surface. The huge branch that had fallen through the roof covered the entire table, and there were broken branches and foliage everywhere.

"Oh…what a mess."

Gabe held her away from him. "Forget that for a minute. Let's check your injuries."

He quickly examined her and looked underneath her bandage. "I don't think it needs stitches, but you should probably see a doctor."

She smiled. "Isn't that what I'm doing right now?"

He stared at her for a moment, and then smiled back. "I guess so. I have a medical kit at home, so I can dress that for you. Now let's get out of here."

And then he lifted her up into his arms as though she were a feather.

"I can walk," she protested.

"Humor me, okay?"

Her legs did feel shaky, so she nodded. Seconds later, he

was striding down the hallway and out the front door. The contractors were all hovering by the bottom steps.

"I'm fine," she assured them when she saw their worried faces.

"Don't go inside," Gabe told the workers. "There could be structural damage. I'll be back soon, so wait here."

She smiled at his bossiness and then dropped her head to his shoulder. It felt nice being in his strong arms. When he rounded the hedge, she noticed how his front door was wide-open, as if he'd left the house in a hurry.

"I really can walk," she said once he'd carried her up the steps.

But he didn't put her down until they reached the kitchen. Then he gently set her to her feet and pulled out a chair. Once she was settled and he'd grabbed a first-aid kit, he undid the makeshift bandage and examined the wound.

"It's not deep," he said, and cleaned the area, applied a small bandage around her forearm and then circled it in plastic wrap. "That should keep it dry when you shower."

"Thanks," she said, and fought the urge to fall into his arms again. "I need to get back to my house and call my insurance company."

"Later," he said. "I'll go and check it out while you rest here."

"There's no need to—"

"There's every need," he said, and grabbed her hand. "You've just been through a frightening ordeal, and you're injured. Plus, there's a great gaping hole in the roof and there could be structural damage to the house."

Lauren ran her free hand down her torn T-shirt and jeans. "I need some fresh clothes, so I'll go home and change and then call the—"

"Stop being so damned obstinate," he said impatiently. "Let me check out the house, and I'll get your clothes while I'm there."

She pulled her hand free. "I'm not sure I want you rummaging through my underwear drawer. It's private and—"

"Lauren, I have seen you naked," he reminded her. "Remember? It's a little late for modesty. Go and take a shower, and I'll be back soon."

"A shower? I don't know why you—"

"Once you look in the mirror, you'll see why," he said, and smiled. "I'll be back soon."

He left the room, and Lauren tried not to be irritated by his high-handedness. She cradled her sore arm and headed for the en-suite bathroom. And worked out why he'd insisted she shower. She was covered in grime and plaster dust. Her face and hair were matted with the stuff, and her clothes were speckled with blood and dirty smudges.

Lauren stripped off the soiled clothes and stepped beneath the warm water, mindful of the plastic-covered bandage. She washed her hair as best she could, and by the time she emerged from the cubicle, wrapped her hair up in a towel and slipped into his bathrobe, she heard him striding down the hallway.

He paused in the doorway carrying a short stack of clothes. "Let me know if you need anything else," he said, and placed them on the bed.

She nodded. "Thank you. How does my house look?"

"Redeemable," he said, and half smiled. "I've told the contractor to tarp the roof so there's no more damage overnight. And I've arranged to have a certified builder assess the damage in the morning. Get dressed, and I'll make you a cup of that tea you like."

Lauren had to admit he'd done a fair job at choosing her clothes. Gray linen pants and a red collared T-shirt, a sensible black bra and brief set and slip-on sandals. As she stepped into the briefs, she didn't want to think about his lean fingers touching her underwear. Gabe's take-charge attitude should have made her as mad as ever, but she was actually grateful for his kindness. What had been a frightening experience was eased by him coming to her rescue. When she was finished dressing, she headed for the kitchen. He'd made tea, as promised, and was staring out the long window, mug in hand.

"I think I inhaled a bucket of plaster dust," she said when she entered the room.

He turned and met her gaze. "If the cough keeps up, let me know."

"I will. Thanks for the tea." She saw her handbag, dusty laptop and house keys on the counter. "Oh, that's good. I wasn't sure the computer survived the tree crashing on top of it."

"It seems okay," he said quietly. "I found your bag but couldn't find your cell phone."

She shrugged. "That's fine. I don't need it, anyhow."

"So how are you feeling now?" he asked.

"Pleased I dived underneath the table."

"Me, too," he said, and set the mug down. "I'd just gotten home when I saw the pulley snap and then saw the branch nosedive into your roof."

"Apparently, that tree was going to mess with the fence," she said, and grinned. "They didn't warn me about what it might do to my house, though."

He chuckled, and the sound warmed her blood. "I'm glad you're okay. I was worried about you."

He sounded uncomfortable saying it, and Lauren tensed. He might have been worried, but he clearly didn't want to be. She'd accused him of being hot and then cold, and that certainly seemed to sum up the way he acted around her.

"Thanks for coming to my rescue," she said as flippantly as she could manage.

His mouth flattened, and he passed her his phone. "You can call your parents if you like. Or your brother."

She shook her head and placed the phone on the table. "They'll only worry."

"Well, they'll know something's up when you stay with them tonight."

"I'm not going anywhere," she said, and pushed her shoulders back. "I'm sleeping in my own bed, in my own house."

"No," he said quietly. "You're not."

"Ah, yes I am."

"I'm not going to argue with you about this, Lauren. You stay with your parents or your brother, or if you like I'll drive you to Cassie's. But you're not spending the night in a potentially compromised building that has a huge hole in the roof."

She crossed her arms. "You don't get to tell me what to do."

"Right now, when you're being stubborn and disagreeable, I'll do whatever I have to do to keep you safe."

His words had *ownership* stamped all over them, and the fact he had the audacity to say such a thing when he'd made it clear they had no future only amplified her resentment. He really needed to stop interfering. Sure, she was grateful he'd gotten her out from under the table, but that didn't give him open season on deciding where she would sleep.

"I'll be perfectly safe."

The pulse in his cheek throbbed. "No, you won't…so you stay with your family, or you can stay here. Those are your only options."

Of all the bossy, arrogant, bullheaded…

"Fine," she said quickly, and saw the startled look on his face. "I'll stay here."

No way…

Gabe's stomach landed at his feet. She wasn't staying with him when she had a bunch of perfectly good relatives to rely on. She was simply being provocative. He was just about to say as much when the challenge in her eyes silenced any protests.

Instead, he called her bluff. "Okay...but you still have to call your parents and tell them what happened."

Her brows came up. "That's interesting coming from a man who won't pick up the telephone to call his own family."

"We're talking about you," he quipped, "not me."

She shrugged. "So where's my bedroom?"

"I'll sleep in the guest room. You can have my room. You'll be more comfortable there."

"Familiar surroundings, you mean?"

His body tensed. "I haven't finished painting in the guest room," he said, and grabbed his cell. "I can order pizza if you're hungry?"

She nodded. "Sure. No anchovies, please. And extra mushrooms."

He half smiled. "Why don't you rest in the living room, and I'll place the order."

She did as he suggested, and once the pizza had been ordered, Gabe grabbed a couple of ginger beers from the refrigerator and headed for the living room. He found her on the sofa, legs curled up, arms crossed, staring at the blank television.

"Everything all right?" he asked, and passed her a bottle.

"Just thinking about my wrecked house."

"It's a house, Lauren," he said quietly, and sat on the other end of the sofa. "Houses can be fixed."

"Not like people, right?" she shot back, and sighed. "Once broken, always broken."

The tremor in her voice made his insides contract. "Is that how you feel?"

"Sometimes," she admitted. "Lately more often than not. I think I just need to...make some changes."

"Changes?"

She raised her shoulders. "I was thinking of selling the store."

He didn't hide his surprise. "That's a bold move. Are you sure it's the right one?"

"Not really," she replied. "I'm not sure of anything. If I do decide to sell, I know my mother will be disappointed. But I don't know how much longer I can keep pretending that it makes me happy. I've been pretending since... since..."

"Since Tim died?"

She nodded slowly. "Yes. Some days I find it so stifling. And then other days I can't believe I'm having such ungrateful thoughts. I mean, what's not to like about being around people who are looking to create the perfect, most special day and then sharing in that joy? But all I feel is tired and weary of plastering on a wide smile every time a bride comes into the store looking for the gown of her dreams."

Her pain reached deep into his soul. "You've had a bad day...don't make a hasty decision when you might not be thinking clearly."

"Spoken from experience?" she asked softly.

"Yes," he replied.

She shrugged. "I won't."

The doorbell rang, and Gabe got to his feet. "Our dinner. Back in a minute."

They ate in the kitchen, and by eight-thirty were lingering over coffee.

"Are you okay?" he asked when he noticed her frowning.

"Tired," she replied. "And sore. I think I strained my back when I darted underneath the table. Which is a small price to pay considering what could have happened."

Gabe pushed his mug aside. "I don't want to remember what I thought when I saw that tree crash."

"I'm glad you were there to rescue me."

Was she? Was he? It seemed as though there was no escaping the pull that drew them together. It had a will of its own, dragging him back toward her at every opportunity.

"Nothing's changed," he said, and hated how cold his voice sounded.

"Everything's changed. I can't pretend and just switch off my emotions."

"Can't? Or won't?"

Her gaze was unwavering. "What are you so afraid of?"

Gabe sucked in a breath. "Hurting you."

"People get hurt all the time. You can't always control it."

"I can try," he said, and stood. "I won't mislead you, Lauren. I won't make promises I can't keep. I've told you how I feel about you and—"

"Actually," she said, cutting him off. "You haven't said how you feel about me at all…only how you feel about relationships and commitment."

Discomfiture snaked up his spine. "It's the same thing."

Her brows rose tellingly. "That's a man's logic," she said, and got to her feet. "And I'm a woman, Gabe. I think and feel deeply. And I know what I want. For the first time in a long time, I actually know what will make me happy. And who."

Guilt pressed onto his shoulders. "Don't pin your hopes on me, Lauren. I can't make you happy…because I can't promise you a future."

She stared at him, eyes glistening. "Is it because you think you might not be able to give me a baby?"

The burn in his stomach intensified. "You can't deny that's important to you."

"It was," she admitted. "It is. But there are other options, like IVF and adoption. I mean, no two people know if they'll be able to produce a child until they try. And you said it was a possibility, not an absolute."

Her relentless logic was butchering him.

"It's just one more complication, Lauren. One that you don't need."

"But I'm right?" she asked. "So now you're hiding behind this idea of potential infertility to keep me or any other woman at arm's length?"

"I'm not hiding. I'm laying out the facts."

"The facts?" she echoed. "You're like a vault when it comes to the facts. Right now, in this moment, you're well and strong and *here*...why isn't that enough?"

"Because it's not. Because it might not last," he replied, frustrated and angry.

"But you don't know what will happen...no one does."

"I know what the medical data says. I know what the odds are of it coming back. If I can stay healthy for five years and not relapse, then I'll consider my options. But until then—"

"Five years?" She cut him off and shook her head. "You can't organize feelings to order like that."

"I can. I will."

"So you plan to avoid getting close to anyone for the next few years just in case you aren't around to seal the deal? That's absurd. What made you so cynical?"

"Facing the prospect of death."

"I don't believe you," she said hauntingly. "There's more to it. You had a career where you saw death all the time, a career that obviously called out to you because you're mentally strong and compassionate and able to deal with grief and despair and hopelessness. I don't believe that all that strength disappeared because you were faced with the challenge of an illness you've now recovered from."

His chest tightened. "I can't talk about—"

"What happened to you?" she pleaded. "Tell me...what happened that made you so determined to be alone?"

Gabe's heart thundered, and he fought the words that

hovered on the end of his tongue. He didn't want to tell her; he didn't want to admit to anything. But the pained, imploring look on her face was suddenly harder to deny than his deep-seated determination to say nothing.

"My dad died when I was seventeen," he said flatly. "And I watched my mom become hollow inside. At first, I watched her become headstrong in her denial and refuse to admit the inevitable. I watched her use every ounce of strength she had to give him hope and keep him alive. I watched her argue with doctors and oncologists about his treatment and try every holistic and natural remedy she could to give him more time. And then when the treatment stopped working and he relapsed, I watched her care for him and feed him and bathe him, and then I watched her cry every day when she thought no one was looking. And when he died, part of her died, too. She was heartbroken. She was sad, and there was nothing anyone could do for her…there was nothing *I* could do for her."

He drew several gulps of air into his lungs. It was the first time he'd said the words. The first time he'd admitted how helpless he'd felt watching his mother fall apart.

"And I'm never going to put anyone through that…not ever."

She shuddered. "So instead you'll shut the world out?"

"Not the world," he said quickly. "Just…"

"Just me?" she asked, eyes glazed. "Or any woman who wants to be with you for more than a one-night stand?"

"Exactly," he said woodenly.

She shook her head. "It wasn't your job to fix your mother. No one can fix that kind of pain…only time can truly heal," she said quietly. "Believe me, I know. If your mother didn't recover, it's not your responsibility or job to question why. And it must be that your dad was the true love of her life."

"Like Tim was yours?"

Did he sound as jealous by that idea as he felt? He didn't want to feel it. Didn't want to think it. Didn't want to be so conflicted and confused that all he wanted to do was haul her into his arms and kiss her over and over and forget every other wretched thought or feeling.

Her mouth softened. "I did love Tim, very much. But I didn't honor that love when I married James. And when my marriage ended, I was determined to find someone who wouldn't make me feel anything that might dishonor those feelings again. And I tried," she said as tears filled her eyes. "And failed."

"And that's exactly why I won't do this, Lauren. That look you have when you talk about Tim... My mom had that same look. You've been through it, too. You know how it feels to lose someone you care about. Why the hell would you potentially put yourself through that again? It doesn't make sense. You need to walk away from this. And me."

"So you're doing this for me. Is that what you're saying?"

He shrugged. "I'm doing this for us both."

She inhaled resignedly. "I'm going to bed. Are you coming?"

Bed? He groaned inwardly. "No."

Her mouth twitched. "You're not going to make love to me tonight?"

Gabe's entire body tightened. She was pure provocation, and he wanted her so much, his blood felt as though it were on fire.

"No." It was close to the hardest thing he'd ever said.

Her eyes shadowed. "Would you just...hold me?"

Pain and longing sat in his gut like a lead weight. But she didn't know what she was asking. If he stayed with her tonight, there would be no turning back. He wanted her... he wanted her so much he ached inside thinking about denying that feeling. But Gabe wouldn't allow that wanting to turn into needing. Needing meant giving everything. Everything meant loving. And that was impossible.

"I can't." His voice sounded hollow and empty. "I can't give you what you want."

She looked at him, and he saw the disappointment and regret in her eyes. She was hurt.

"No, I guess you can't," she said, and left the room.

Chapter Twelve

"And that's it?"

Lauren dropped her gaze to the floor. If she kept looking at Cassie and Mary-Jayne, they'd see the tears in her eyes. And she wouldn't cry anymore. She'd cried enough over lost love throughout the years. She'd cried for Tim. She'd cried when he'd finally told her he was dying and wouldn't be able to give her the future he'd promised. She'd cried over his grave and in the years since. She'd even cried for James when he'd walked out the door. She'd cried for lost dreams and for the children she'd never borne.

And not once, during all those tears and anguish, did she ever think she'd love again. Nor did she want to. She'd planned on friendship and companionship and then marriage and children to help ease her aching heart. And instead had tumbled headlong into something that was all desire and heat and a longing so intense it physically pained her. She loved Gabe. And she knew, deep down to her soul, that it was the one love she would never recover from.

But she had to try.

And she would.

"That's it," she replied, and pretended to enjoy the glass of wine she'd been cradling for the best part of an hour. She managed a smile. "Looks like I'm back to trawling ReliableBores.com."

Mary-Jayne made a huffing sound. "Did he give you a reason?"

Sure he did. But Lauren would never betray Gabe's confidence and tell them about his illness. Now she had to concentrate on forgetting all about her fledging feelings and put Gabe Vitali out of her mind. And show a little more enthusiasm for her friends' company. But she wasn't in the mood for a Friday-evening movie and junk-food marathon. She simply wanted to lick her wounds in private.

"Don't forget it's my sister's birthday party tomorrow night," Mary-Jayne reminded them. "I'll pick you both up."

Lauren nodded and noticed that Cassie, who still hadn't heard from Doug, looked about as unenthused as she felt. An evening with Scott and Evie Jones was one thing… knowing Gabe would be there, too, was another thing altogether. However, she was determined to put on a brave face and go. Avoiding Gabe was pointless. They shared several of the same friends and were bound to run into one another occasionally. She might be able to steer clear of him over the hedge that separated their homes, but becoming a hermit to her friends wasn't an option.

"How's the house look?" Cassie asked.

"The repairs will take the best part of the weekend, but I should be back in by Tuesday."

"Well, you can stay here as long as you like," her friend offered.

And she was glad she had such loyal friends. She'd gone to bed the night before with a broken heart and awoke with more resolve than she knew she possessed. Gabe was gone by the time she pulled herself out of bed, and had left a cursory note telling her a builder would be at her house at seven-thirty to check for structural damage. By eight she was back inside her own house, cleaning up with the help of the fencing contractor and his crew, who'd arrived with sheepish faces and good intentions. And while the repairs to the roof were being done, she'd stay with Cassie and try to stop thinking about Gabe.

"Thanks, I appreciate it."

"That's what friends are for," Cassie assured her, then smiled. "You know, there's this man at work I think you might like."

Lauren groaned. "A blind date? Ah, no thanks."

"What's the harm? He's nice. He's in the pathology department. Want me to set you up?"

"No chance."

On Saturday morning, Lauren headed to the store early. She gave her mother an abridged version of what had happened with the house, leaving out how she'd stayed at Gabe's that night and only telling her she was bunking in with Cassie until the repairs were done. She didn't mention her thoughts about selling the store. She'd think about that later. When her heart wasn't breaking. When she was whole and was certain she'd finished crying wasted tears.

Late that afternoon, Lauren dressed in a pale lemon sundress in filmy rayon that tied at her nape. The garment fitted neatly over the bodice and flared from the waist. She matched it with a pair of silver heels and kept her hair loose around her shoulders. Mary-Jayne picked her up at six, and since Cassie had decided to give the party a miss, they drove straight to Dunn Inn. The big A-framed home was set back from the road, and the gardens always reminded

Lauren of something out of an old fairy story. There was a wishing well in the center of the yard, surrounded by cobbled paths and tall ferns, and it had been a bed and breakfast for over a decade.

Gabe's car wasn't out front, and she heaved a relieved sigh. She grabbed Evie's birthday gift from the backseat and followed Mary-Jayne inside. Evie was in the kitchen, as was Grace. Lauren had always envied the three sisters' relationship. They were as different as night and day and yet shared a formidable bond. Of course, she adored her brother, but sometimes wished she'd had a sister, too.

"Scott's running an errand," Evie explained, and Lauren wondered if she imagined how the other woman glanced in her direction just a little longer than expected. "He'll be back soon."

Mary-Jayne laughed. "Oh, with some big birthday surprise for you?"

Evie raised her steeply arched brows. "Well, it's certainly a surprise. Not for me, though. And since I'm not sure I really want to be celebrating the fact I'm only two years off turning forty, I'm more than happy about that."

"The gifts are all on the buffet in the front living room," Grace said as she cradled Evie's six-month-old daughter in her arms.

Her sister-in-law was glowing, and Lauren wondered if she was pregnant. It would certainly explain why her brother had sounded so chipper on the phone that morning when he'd called after hearing about her tree mishap from her mother. She was achingly happy for Cameron and knew he deserved every ounce of happiness that was in his life. But part of her envied him, too. He'd put his heart on the line when he'd pursued Grace, and it had paid off.

Not like me....

Her heart was well and truly smashed. Gabe was out of reach. As unattainable as some remote planet. He'd made it abundantly clear that he wasn't interested. He'd rejected her, wholly and completely. And she had to stop wasting her energy hoping he'd come around. There would be no fairy-tale ending.

Lauren offered to take the gifts into the living room and left the sisters alone to catch up. The big room was formal and furnished with a long leather chaise and twin heavy brocade sofas. A collection of Evie's artwork covered the walls, and a thick rug lay in front of the fireplace and hearth.

She'd just laid the gifts out when she heard the wide French doors rattle. A second later, Gabe was in the room. In black trousers and white shirt, he looked so handsome, it was impossible to arrest the breathless gasp that escaped her throat. But he looked a little tired, too, and she wondered if he'd had as much trouble sleeping as she'd had. She almost wished sleeplessness upon him. She wanted to share everything with him...including her misery.

He didn't say anything. He only looked at her, taking his time to rake his stare from her sandaled feet to her freshly washed hair. A gust of awareness swept into the room like a seductive wind, and she couldn't have moved even if she'd tried. Heat coursed up her limbs and hit her low in the belly. In a flash of a second she remembered every touch, every kiss, every moment of their lovemaking. And she knew, by the scorching intensity of his gaze, that he was remembering it, too.

It was hard to stop from rushing into his arms. Because they were the arms she loved. She wondered how it had happened...how she'd managed to fall in love with a man who didn't love her in return. Who wouldn't risk loving her in return. A man who was everything she'd sworn off and yet was everything she craved. A man who openly offered her nothing but heartache.

"Lauren," he said finally, breaking the thick silence. "You look lovely."

She swallowed hard and shrugged. "Thank you."

"How are you feeling? Is your arm getting better?"

"Yes," she said, and touched the narrow bandage. "Healing well."

"How's the house?"

"Good," she replied. "Actually, I wanted to thank you for getting the builder to come around and assess the place. He's been very accommodating and will have the repairs finished by next week."

"No problem. He's the father of one of the kids in the junior lifeguard program at the surf club. He was happy to help out."

"Well, I appreciate your concern. I didn't see your truck out front so I wasn't sure you would be here today."

"I'm parked out back," he explained. "If you'd rather I left, then I'll go."

"No," she said quickly. "It's fine," she lied, dying inside. "It's Evie's birthday, and Scott is your cousin. You should be here with your family."

He stepped closer. "I've been thinking about you."

She shrugged. "I can't imagine why."

His gaze was unrelenting. "We left things badly the other day and I—"

"It's fine," she assured him with way more bravado than she felt. "You said what you had to say. I'm over it."

I'm over you....

Liar.

He nodded slowly. "That's...good. You know, I never planned on hurting you."

Humiliation coursed through her blood, and she had to dig herself out of the hole she was in. "You didn't, so spare yourself the concern. I'm perfectly okay. We had one night together. The sex was great. The pancakes were not so great." She shrugged again and plastered on a tight smile as she counted off a few fingers. "And I'm back to day three of my new vow of celibacy."

"So…you're okay?"

Her smile broadened. "Never better. Don't worry on my account, Gabe. We had sex…it's not a big deal. People have sex all the time. We had an itch, we scratched it."

His mouth thinned. "An itch? Is that what it was?"

"Sure," she said, and shrugged. "What else? I mean, we really don't know one another very well, and we always seem to end up arguing. It's better we slept together early on rather than drag the whole thing out for an age. My plans haven't changed, and yours seem set in stone… so no harm done."

He stared at her, long and hard, and finally he crossed his arms and shook his head. "I don't believe you, Lauren. I think…I think you're saying what you imagine I want to hear."

She laughed loudly. "Maybe I just wanted to get laid… like you did."

"Is that what you think I wanted?" he asked quietly. "To get laid?"

"Sure," she replied, and shrugged. "You told me as much that night you came over for dinner, remember? You called me Commitment 101 and said you have casual and meaningless sex."

His brows came up. "I said that?"

"Words to that effect."

He smiled. "Well, I haven't had as much meaningless sex as you've clearly been imagining. And before you go accusing me of doing that with you, be assured there was nothing meaningless to me about the night we spent together. You told me you don't make love casually, and I believe that." He said the words with such arrogant confidence, she wanted to slug him. "But I think you're hurt and I think you're angry. And I also think—"

"And I think you're the most conceited jerk of all time," she said hotly, cutting him off. A door closed in the house, and she heard voices, but Lauren pressed on, battling with the humiliating fury she felt in her heart. He didn't want her. He didn't need her. Why couldn't he simply leave her alone? "I don't care how much I want to get laid in the future, I will steer well clear of your bed. One night in the sack with you isn't enough to—"

Lauren stopped ranting when she heard someone clearing their throat and noticed that three people were standing in the doorway. It was Scott and two others. A man, tall and handsome with fair hair and blue eyes just like Gabe's, and a woman whose eyes were equally as blue and who looked to be around sixty. She heard Gabe groan as he turned on his heels and faced the group.

When he spoke, Lauren almost fainted on the spot.

"Hi, Mom."

Seeing Claire Vitali in the doorway, with his brother Aaron hovering close by, was enough to quell any urge he had to kiss Lauren's amazing mouth. Since he'd walked into the room and spotted her by the buffet, it was all he'd wanted to do. With her temper flared and her cheeks ablaze with color, he'd never seen her look more beautiful or more desirable. But she was hurting, too, and even though she denied it, Gabe knew he was responsible for the unhappiness in her eyes. He hated that he'd done that…even though he felt certain it was for the best.

The group moved into the room, and before he had a chance to make introductions, his mother was clutching at him in a fierce and long embrace. Once she'd finished hugging, she kissed his cheek and stepped back.

"It's good to see you, Gabriel," she said, using his full name for deliberate effect, and smiled.

Despite his shock, he was genuinely pleased to see his parent. "You, too, Mom."

His mother noticed Lauren immediately and held out her hand. "Hello, I'm Claire Vitali."

Lauren took her hand and introduced herself. "It's nice to meet you."

Gabe saw the gleam in his mother's eyes. "And you."

"Well, I'll leave you all to catch up," Lauren said, and moved across the room as if her soles were on fire. He noticed she smiled at Aaron and Scott on her way out but didn't spare him a glance.

"I'll go, too," Scott said, and grinned.

"Yeah," Gabe said. "Thanks so much for the heads-up."

His cousin shrugged. "Our mothers swore me to secrecy. And don't be too long. It's my wife's birthday, and there's cake."

Once he was gone, Aaron stepped toward him. "That's one pretty girl," his brother said with a grin, and went for a bear hug. Gabe ignored the comment about Lauren and hugged him back.

When the hugging was over and they were settled on the two sofas, he asked the obvious question. "So what are you two doing here?"

"I'm here because she insisted I come," Aaron said, and grinned.

"I wanted to see my son," his mother replied. "And since you weren't returning my calls…"

Gabe glanced at his older brother, looking his usually cocky self on the opposite sofa, and scowled. "I did text and say I was busy."

"Mom didn't believe me," Aaron said, and grinned again. "She wanted to see for herself."

He looked to his mother. "See what?"

"I needed to make sure you were okay," she said, and gave him a look of concern.

"I'm fine," he said. "As you can see."

His mother's mouth thinned. "Are you really? You can tell me if you're not."

"You came all this way because you thought I'd had some kind of relapse?"

She sighed crossly. "I came all this way because you're my son, and you and your brothers and sister are the most important thing in my life. I won't apologize for caring."

Guilt pressed between his ribs. "I'm sorry I worried you. But I'm fine."

"You don't look fine," she said, and frowned. His mother never was one to pull punches. "You look tired and annoyed, and you're clearly not happy that we've turned up unannounced. So what's going on with you?"

Sometimes Gabe wished he came from one of those families where everyone didn't know everyone else's business. Was there such a thing as caring too much? When he'd been diagnosed with lymphoma, his mother and siblings had closed ranks around him, almost to the point of smothering him with concern. And it hadn't taken long for resentment to set in. Since then, they'd treated him differently, and it irritated the hell out of him. It was as though they'd wanted to wrap him in cotton wool and *fix* everything.

"Nothing," he assured her, feeling about sixteen years old. "Everything's fine. I'm healthy. I have a job I like, friends… You don't need to worry, Mom. I'm a grown man, and I can take care of myself."

"I'll always worry," she said, still looking grim. "It's a given that a mother worries about her children, regardless of how old they are." She sighed and patted his arm affectionately. "But if you say you're fine…then I believe you. You still look tired, though."

"I'm just not sleeping great at the moment. Otherwise, I'm in perfect health and have the results of my latest tests to prove it. Please, stop fretting."

"So," Aaron said, and stretched back in the sofa. "You're fine. Which doesn't explain why you've been avoiding our calls for the past month or so." His brows rose questioningly. "What's the story with the pretty blonde with the big brown eyes who you clearly got into bed but who now wants nothing to do with you?"

"Aaron," their mother chastised. "That's enough."

Gabe's mouth pressed tight. "My relationship with Lauren is no one's business and I don't—"

"Relationship?" His brother laughed and cut him off. "Ha...of course. Now I get it." Aaron propped forward on the seat and grinned broadly. He looked at their mother. "Mom, he's not sick...he's *lovesick*."

Gabe found the urge to crash tackle his big-mouthed brother. "Shut up."

"Aaron." Their mom said his brother's name again, this time quietly. "Go and eat some cake. I'd like to talk to your brother alone."

"I'm right," Aaron said with a grin as he stood. "I know I'm right."

Once Aaron left, Gabe faced his mother's stare. "Is that true?" she asked gently.

"Is what true?"

She made a face. "Lauren... Are you in love with her?"

Gabe got to his feet and paced around the sofa. "No."

"But you're involved with her?"

"Not exactly. It's complicated," he said, and shrugged. "And I don't want to talk about it."

"Well, that's always been your problem, really...not talking," his mom said, and sighed. "Just like your father. Not talking about your illness...not talking about what happened at the hospital when you went back to work…not talking about why you broke up with Mona…not talking about why you needed to put an ocean between your old life and your new one."

His shoulders tensed. "You know why I left."

"Because you blamed yourself for that woman and her baby dying," she said gently. "Even though it wasn't your fault. Even though you weren't there."

"I *should* have been there. I was on duty."

"You were sick," his mother reminded him.

"Yes," he said hollowly. "I was. And I went back too soon. I did everything I would have told a patient to *not* do. I ignored what was best and did exactly what I wanted, and because of that a young woman and her baby died. I am to blame, Mom. It doesn't matter how many times I try to get it clear in my head, or how often I'm told the inquiry didn't find me culpable." He pointed to his temple. "In here I feel the blame. In here I see her husband weeping over her body. Because I was arrogant and thought I could trick my broken body into being what it once was." He sighed heavily. "But it's not. And it might never be. I won't pretend anymore. And I certainly won't drag anyone else into that place if I do end up back where I was."

His mother's eyes glistened. "You mean Lauren?"

"I mean anyone," he said pointedly. "I saw what it did to you, Mom…watching Dad slowly fade away. It was hard to sit back and for a time watch you fade away, too."

"Gabe, I didn't—"

"We should get back to the party," he said, and held out his arm. "Before that lousy brother of mine eats all the birthday cake."

She blinked a couple of times. They weren't done. But his mother knew not to push too much. Gabe led her into the dining room and noticed that everyone was there, standing around the table as Evie prepared to blow out the birthday candles...everyone except Lauren.

Had she left?

He ducked out of the room and headed outside. She was in the front yard, standing on the cobbled pathway by the wishing well, partially hidden by large ferns, arms crossed and clearly deep in thought. Everything about her reached him deep down, into a place he'd never let anyone go.

Are you in love with her?

His mother's words came rushing back. He'd denied it. Because he didn't want to face what it would mean to truly love a woman like Lauren. Aaron had called him love-sick, and in a way that's exactly how he felt. He couldn't define it, couldn't put into words what he was feeling when he was around her. It was like a fever that wouldn't break. A pain that wouldn't abate. His chest hurt simply thinking about her. And his damned libido seemed to be on a kind of constant red alert.

Was that love?

He hoped not. He didn't want it to be. He was no good for Lauren.

"Are you making wishes?" he asked as he approached.

She shook her head. "I don't think I believe in them."

"You're going to miss out on cake," he said.

She turned her head sideways. "I'm going to skip the cake. And the party."

"Are you planning on walking home?" he asked, stepping a little closer.

"It's not far," she replied. "A few blocks."

"In those heels?" He stared at her feet for a moment. "I'll drive you home if that's what you want."

"No," she said quietly. "You should stay here with your family." She uncrossed her arms and turned toward him. "Your mother seems nice."

"She is nice."

"And clearly worried about you," she said, and smiled wryly. "I told you to call her."

Gabe shrugged. "I know you did. I should have listened. She was convinced I had...you know...relapsed."

"Well, she must be relieved to know you're fine. And I'm sorry if your mother and brother overheard our conversation before," she said, and Gabe noticed her cheeks were pinkish. "I shouldn't have lost my temper."

"My mom's cool. And don't worry about Aaron. He's a jerk, too," he said, and grinned a little. "You'd probably like him."

Lauren rolled her eyes. "I've decided to give up on handsome and charming men. Too much trouble."

"Maybe there's something safe in that middle road you were looking for."

"Maybe," she agreed. "Anyhow, I'm going home now."

Gabe reached for her instinctively. He took her hand and wrapped his fingers around hers. "I'm...I'm sorry, Lauren."

She didn't pull away. She didn't move. She only looked up at him, and in the fading afternoon light, he could see every feature. The morning after the night they'd made love, he'd watched her sleep, and in that time he'd memorized every line and curve of her face. He wanted to make love to her again. And again. He wanted to hold her in his arms and kiss her beautiful mouth. But she wasn't his to kiss.

"I know you are," she said so quietly, her voice whispered along the edge of the breeze. "I am, too. I'm sorry you think you're not worth the risk. And I'm sorry you think I'm not strong enough to handle whatever might happen. I guess after what happened with Tim, you have your reasons for believing that. But you're doing exactly what Tim did. He didn't trust me enough to try.... He didn't trust me enough to let me in and share the time he had...and you don't trust me, either."

Gabe's insides jerked. "It's not about trust."

"It is." She pulled her hand from his and reached up to gently touch his face, eyes glistening. "But do you want to know something, Gabe? I would have rather had five years, one year, one month with you...than a lifetime with someone else."

Chapter Thirteen

Lauren moved back into her house on Wednesday afternoon, and since the new fence was now complete, she had less chance of seeing Gabe. Which was exactly what she wanted.

She also made a few decisions. She talked with her mother about The Wedding House and agreed that they'd look to finding a buyer within the next twelve months if she was still keen to sell. In the meantime, Lauren had decided to cut back her hours at the store and return part-time to college to get her accounting degree.

And after much convincing from her meddling, albeit well-meaning friends, she agreed to go on a date with Cassie's pathologist on Friday night. She also made a commitment to walk Cassie's dog, Mouse, since her friend was still feeling the effects of her appendectomy, and at nearly five months pregnant, wasn't keen to be on the end of the leash of the huge Harlequin Great Dane. He was well mannered, though, and incredibly quiet and not unruly like Jed.

On Friday morning, she took him for a long walk, and was heading back along the pathway when she saw Megan jogging toward her. The teen's long limbs stretched out, and her tiny sports shorts molded her toned thighs. Lauren felt about as sporty as an old shoe in her baggy cotton shorts and sensible racer-back T-shirt when the girl came up to her.

"Hey, there," Megan said cheerfully. "Nice dog."

"Thanks," she said, and tried to be as equally cheerful.

"So," the other girl said, jogging on the spot. "Are you the reason why Gabe's in such a bad mood?"

Lauren's skin prickled. "I don't know what you mean."

She shrugged. "It was just something my sister said. But she can be pretty catty when she wants to be. She had this idea that you and Gabe were together."

"No, we're not."

Megan grinned. "Have you met his brother? He's hot. But then, I've always had a thing for blonds. Anyhow, if you're not the reason why he's in a bad mood, someone is, 'cause he's been unbearable all week." Megan laughed shrilly. "Gotta run. See ya!"

She watched the other girl jog away, and then turned Mouse back onto the path. She was about twenty feet from passing alongside the surf club when she spotted Gabe's brother outside the building, phone pressed to his ear. He was handsome, she thought, but not as classically good-looking as his younger brother. Lauren was hoping to pass by unnoticed, but he waved to her when he realized who she was.

Seconds later, he walked over. "Nice to see you again," he said, and smiled. "Although I don't think we were actually introduced. I'm Aaron. That's some dog you have there."

"He's on loan from a friend. So are you enjoying Crystal Point?"

"I like the scenery," he said, and grinned. "And nice weather. It's a lot like California."

She asked him about his twin sons, and was about to excuse herself when she saw Gabe standing on the second-story balcony, watching them. Or more to the point, glaring at them.

"Uh-oh," Aaron said, and waved to his brother. "He doesn't look happy. Can't figure why. Can you?" he asked with a devilish grin.

Heat seeped up her neck, and Lauren shrugged. "No idea."

"He can be a little uptight about some things."

She'd never considered Gabe to be uptight. Bossy and hardheaded, perhaps. And stubborn. And handsome and sexy, and she'd always thought him to be rather charming and easygoing. Stupidly, she didn't like that his brother was so openly criticizing him.

"I suppose we can all be like that," she said quietly. "Under certain circumstances."

He laughed loudly. "Ah, so you, too, huh?"

"Me, too, what?" she asked, puzzled.

He laughed again. "Nothing…just go easy on him, okay? He's been through a lot. And I don't think he quite knows what to do about you, Lauren."

Reject me…that's what.

She'd laid her heart on the line. She'd told him how she felt in the garden at Dunn Inn and he'd only turned around and walked away. No words. No comfort. No acknowledgment.

His silence had told her all she needed to know.

"Oh, I'm pretty sure he does. Nice talking with you. So long."

She walked off and felt Gabe's gaze follow her the entire way up the path until she disappeared from his view. He could stare all he wanted. She'd had nearly a week to pull herself together and had so far had done a good job. He was out of her thoughts.

Now all she had to do was get him out of her heart, as well.

Gabe missed Lauren like crazy. He missed talking to her. He missed how the scent of her perfume always seemed to linger on his clothes for ages after they'd spent time together. And he missed kissing her.

And he hated that he'd hurt her.

I would have rather have had five years, one year, one month with you...than a lifetime with someone else.

Her words haunted him. They were honest and heartfelt and much more than he was worthy of. And he'd been so tempted to take what she offered. More than tempted. He'd wanted it. Longed for it. *Ached* for it.

He'd wanted to wrap her in his arms and hold her there forever.

Except...he might not have forever to offer her. And she deserved that. She deserved more than an empty promise and his broken, defective body.

He headed back downstairs and started work. It was mind-numbing admin stuff, but at least it kept him busy. And gave him a chance to stop thinking about Lauren.

"That's one seriously gorgeous woman."

Gabe turned around. Aaron was hovering by the door. He knew his brother was talking about Lauren. "Aren't you supposed to be packing for your flight tomorrow?"

"Change of plans," he quipped. "Mom and I were just talking... We're staying another week."

Gabe groaned to himself. Another week? He wasn't sure he'd cope with another week of his well-meaning mother and annoying older sibling. "Why? Don't you have a life and two kids to get back to?"

Aaron smiled, walked into the office and plunked into a

chair. "You know very well that my ex-wife has the boys, and my business partner is running things while I'm away. And anyway, I wouldn't miss this chance to see you squirm for anything."

Gabe called him an unflattering name and pretended to work.

"You didn't answer my question," Aaron said.

He stared at the paperwork on his desk. "It wasn't a question," he reminded his brother. "It was a statement. And I'm not squirming."

Aaron laughed. "Oh, you sure as hell are. And I must say she's very pretty and kind of wholesome looking...but sexy underneath that whole girl-next-door thing, if you know what I mean."

Gabe knew exactly what he meant. He jerked his head up. "Haven't you got somewhere else to be? Someone else to irritate?"

Aaron linked his hands behind his head and stretched. "Nope...just you."

"I'm working."

"You're ignoring my question...got it bad, huh?"

Gabe scowled. "What I've got is work to do and no time to waste. I'll see you tonight, around six."

His family was staying at Dunn Inn for the duration of their trip, since Gabe had insisted his house wasn't ready for guests, and the B and B was more comfortable. But he'd put off having them around all week until they'd invited themselves over for dinner that night.

His brother left shortly afterward, and Gabe spent the day moving from bad mood to foul mood and in no particular order. Not even the news that he'd been successful in his interview with the hospital had lightened his spirits. There were licenses and insurances to renew, but he'd been offered a job in the E.R. and would start the following month. It meant he had time to hand in his resignation and help find a replacement.

By the time he returned home, it was well after five. He took a quick shower, dressed in jeans and T-shirt and was just marinating the steaks when he heard Scott's dual-cab truck pull up outside. He headed outside and walked down the steps. By the time he reached his brother and mother, another car had pulled up next door. He could see over the fence, and when he spotted Lauren walking down her driveway and then the male driver of the car get out, Gabe's body stilled. They were saying hello. She was smiling. The man opened the passenger door and she got into the car.

Aaron was now out of the truck and was also watching. He clamped Gabe on the shoulder and chuckled. "Looks as though you've got yourself some competition."

"Don't be an ass," Gabe said, and opened the door for their mother.

He greeted his mom and kept one eye on the car as it drove off down the cul-de-sac.

She's on a date....

It shouldn't have made him madder than hell. It shouldn't have made him feel anything. He'd made the rules. She'd opened her heart, and he'd refused to take it. But a date?

He was burning inside just thinking about it.

Over dinner, he stayed silent and let his brother and mom talk. Tension pressed down on his shoulders, and he couldn't quell the uneasy feeling in his gut. He'd told her to find someone else, and she'd done exactly as he'd suggested. It should have eased the guilt. But it didn't. It only amplified the confusion and discontent rumbling through his system and settling directly in the region of his heart.

When Aaron took a phone call and wandered off to the living room for some privacy, his mother cornered Gabe by the kitchen counter.

"So now that you've had a few days to calm down, would you like to tell me about Lauren?"

He shook his head. "No."

His mother sighed. "Do you know what I think? I think you're very much in love with her, and it scares you like you've never been scared before."

I'm not in love with her. I'm not in love with her. I'm not in love with her....

"Nonsense," he said, and started stacking plates in the dishwasher.

"Are you worried she'll leave like Mona did, should your health change?"

"Lauren is nothing like Mona," he replied, and continued stacking. "Actually, I'm concerned she'll do exactly the opposite."

His mother shook her head. "Gabe, isn't that her choice to make?"

"Not if I can help it." He straightened and placed his hands on the counter. "Please stay out of it, Mom. That means no interfering, no meddling... Promise me you'll just leave it alone."

"I can't do that," she said, and smiled. "When one of my kids is in trouble, I'll always interfere."

"I'm not in trouble," he insisted. "And I know what I'm doing. She's grieved for one man already. I won't be responsible for her having to do that over another."

"Another man? Who?"

He briefly explained about Tim. "Now, can we drop it?"

His mother nodded. "Yes, of course."

Gabe made coffee, and when Aaron returned, they sat around the table for a while, telling old tales about things they'd done as kids. Like the time Aaron got caught making out with the local minister's daughter, or when geeky, sixteen-year-old Luca got suspended from math club because he'd followed Gabe and Aaron and gotten a tattoo on his arm. The stories made him laugh and put him in a marginally better mood. He waved them off at nine-thirty but was back on the porch fifteen minutes later when he spotted a car return next door.

She got out and walked up the driveway as the car pulled away. So her date didn't see her to the door. *Schmuck.* Mounting dislike and rage festered in his gut for a few more minutes, and before he had a chance to stop himself, Gabe was striding around the fence, the hedge and then through the gate and up the steps.

He tapped on the door and waited. He heard her heels clicking on the timber floor, and when she pulled the door open, she looked genuinely surprised to see him.

"Oh…Gabe."

He shifted on his feet. She was so beautiful. Her hair was down, framing her perfectly lovely face, highlighting the deep caramel eyes that haunted him. She wore a little black dress that flipped over her hips and made every ounce of desire and longing he possessed surge to the surface in a wave.

"Who the hell was that?" he demanded once she'd opened the security door.

She moved back a little. "You mean my date?"

"Yeah," he shot back, so agitated he could barely get the word out. "Your *date.*"

She actually smiled. Like she thought him hilarious. Or the biggest fool of all time. Or both. "His name is Steve. Although I'm not quite sure how that's any of your business."

It wasn't. *She was on a date with someone named Steve.* Steve who? He hated the name, anyhow. *Forget about it… she can do whatever she likes. And with whomever she likes.* But be damned if the very idea of that didn't make every part of his flesh and bones ache.

"I was only…" He stopped, realizing nothing he could say would make him look like anything other than exactly what he was—a stupidly jealous idiot. It was a sobering realization. Had he ever been jealous before? Had he ever cared enough about anyone to garner such an emotional response?

No. Never.

I think you're very much in love with her, and it scares you like you've never been scared before....

His mother's words beat around in his head.

She made an impatient sound. "Goodbye, Gabe."

He didn't move. He stared at her. Long and deep. And the more he stared, the more he knew her impatience increased. And before he had a chance to question why, he reached out and pulled her close. She looked startled for a microsecond and then tilted her head and glared up at him. Body to body, breath to breath, Gabe experienced a connection with her that was so intense, so acute, it almost knocked him unconscious. Had her date kissed her? Had another man kissed those lips he'd somehow come to think of as his own? His arms tightened around her frame, drawing her against him so intimately, he could feel every lovely rise and curve.

She shook her head. "Don't you so much as think about—"

He claimed her lips, driving his own to hers with blatant passion and little finesse. He found her tongue and toyed with it, drawing it into an erotic dance as old as time. It took her seconds to respond, and she kissed him back, winding her tongue around his, and the sensation pitched an arrow of intense pleasure from his mouth to his chest and stomach and then directly to his groin. He urged her hips closer and groaned. She felt so good, and he wanted her so much. He wanted to strip her naked and feel every luscious curve and dip of her body. He wanted to lose himself in her sweet loving and forget he couldn't give her what she deserved.

Gabe was about to ease them both across the threshold

when she suddenly wrenched free. She pulled away from him and stumbled back on unsteady feet, dragging in big gulps of air.

She pressed the back of her fingers against her mouth. "Don't do that again."

"Lauren, I—"

"Leave me alone, Gabe. Don't kiss me. Don't touch me. Don't come over. Don't call. Don't so much as leave me a note in my letterbox. I'm done. You got that? *Done*."

Then she closed the door in his face.

Lauren didn't sleep that night. She tossed in her bed and stared at the ceiling. How *dare* Gabe turn up on her doorstep and demand to know who she'd been out with. How *dare* he act all jealous and wounded. And how *dare* he kiss her like that! It was a kiss that had *possession* stamped all over it. And he didn't own her. Her broken heart had now turned into an angry one. He'd forfeited any rights she may have given him. She'd date whoever she wanted to. Even Steve, who had been the perfect gentleman over dinner and was polite and friendly and had done all the right things for a first date. And since he'd called her only ten minutes after dropping her off and asked if he could see her again, he was clearly emotionally available. Unlike Gabe, who obviously only wanted to kiss her and confuse her. So maybe Steve didn't make her pulse race.... He might, over time.

She finally dropped off to sleep after two and woke up with a headache. Saturday morning was busy at the store. Lauren had a gown fitting around ten and put on a smile when the exuberant client arrived with her wedding party. The dress was a beautiful concoction of ivory organza and lace, and it fitted the bride like a glove. By midday the last client had left, and Lauren closed the doors while her mother attended to the cashiering.

"Everything all right?"

Irene Jakowski was too smart to fool. Lauren had been on autopilot for most of the day, doing and saying the right thing, when inside she was confused and hurting and angry.

"Fine, Matka," she said when her mother repeated her question.

Her mother nodded and touched her arm. "There's someone special out there for you, I know it."

Lauren sighed. "I think I've already had my someone special."

"You mean Tim?" her mother asked. "Are you sure about that?"

She frowned just a little. "Of course. You know what he meant to me."

"I know," Irene said. "But you were young when you met, and teenage love can sometimes have you looking through rose-colored glasses."

"Are you saying Tim might not have been as perfect as I imagine he was?"

Irene nodded. "He was a nice young man, and I know you were compatible in many ways. And you might have been happy together. But sometimes easy isn't necessarily what will *keep* you happy. You married James on the rebound. All I'm saying is don't *settle* simply because you think you have to. And not when something wonderful might be within your reach."

She knew what her mother was suggesting. In her mother's romantic eyes, Steve was settling, and Gabe was Mr. Wonderful. "It was one date, Matka," she reminded her. "A nice date, but one date."

"That's how it starts."

No, it had started with heated looks, an argument and an unexpected fall into a swimming pool. Now she had to get him out of her system, her head and her heart.

"I'm not going to settle, I promise you. I've had enough of thinking I want the middle road. I told myself I would be happy with that because I felt so guilty about marrying James. I mean, the way I did it, the way I had everything the same as when I'd planned to marry Tim, only the groom was different. *That's* when I settled, when I married a man I didn't love because I was so wrapped up in having a big wedding. And it didn't make either of us happy. If my brief relationship with Gabe has shown me anything, it's that I want to be *in love.* Truly, madly and deeply. Because I know what it feels like now, and anything less simply won't be enough."

There were tears in her mother's eyes when she'd finished speaking. "I'm glad to hear you say that. I'm glad to hear you want to be happy. After Tim's death and then with James...I wondered if you'd ever risk your heart again. But you did. And I'm very proud of you."

Lauren shuddered out a long breath. "I did risk my heart, Matka. He just didn't want it."

On Saturday night, Gabe paced the rooms of his house like a caged bear. She'd gone out again. The same car had arrived to collect her at six o'clock. It was now close to ten, and she wasn't home. He tried painting the last of the bedrooms to take his mind off Lauren and her date and imagining her doing who knows what. When that didn't work, he poured bourbon he didn't drink, ordered pizza he didn't eat and ignored the two calls from Aaron on his cell.

He fell asleep on the sofa and woke up at midnight with a cramp in his neck. The lights were off next door and the realization that Lauren might have decided to stay out all night cut through him with the precision of a knife. By morning, Gabe was so wound up that he pulled on sweats and sneakers and ran for a solid hour, only caving when he got a stitch in his side. He jogged home, showered and changed into worn jeans and T-shirt and downed two cups of strong coffee.

When his mother arrived at ten, minus Aaron, he knew he was in for a sermon. He sat in the kitchen, cradling a mug of coffee and waited for it.

And got it in spades.

"I've been talking with Irene Jakowski," she said so matter-of-factly, she got his immediate attention. "And we've decided that we need to knock some sense into the pair of you."

Gabe actually laughed. "Mom, I think you and Mrs. Jakowski should stop colluding and accept the inevitable."

"And what's that? You're unhappy. Lauren's unhappy. The only thing that's inevitable is that it's going to stay that way unless you do something about it."

"She's moved on," he said, and pushed the mug aside. "Which is how it should be."

"Stubborn as a mule," his mother said, and tutted. "Just like your father."

"Realistic and sensible," he replied, and half smiled. "Just like you."

"Gabriel," she said with deliberate emphasis. "I'm going to say something I never thought I would ever have to say to you." She drew in a long breath. "Stop being such a coward."

"Mom, I—"

"All your life you've done the right thing. As a child, you never got into any serious trouble. You did well at school. You studied hard. You stayed away from the wrong crowds. You really were a pillar of strength when your dad died. Afterward, you pulled the family together. You were the glue, Gabe. I was so very proud when you got into medical school and then even more so when you became such a wonderful doctor. But I was so busy being proud, I failed to see that I'd relied on you too much."

His throat thickened. "You didn't, Mom."

"I did," she said. "And all that responsibility took a

heavy toll on you. While Aaron was acting wild and chasing girls and Luca was sticking his head into a computer to avoid thinking about what we'd all lost, you worked hard and got on with things. And I think a part of you closed down because of that responsibility. Aaron is charming and says whatever's on his mind, and Luca is all moody and mysterious and cross...but you don't let anything or anyone touch you."

She sighed and reached across the table to grasp his hand. "You got sick. And you should have shouted and complained and blamed something or someone...but you never did. You kept it inside and locked everyone else out. We were all falling apart at the idea of losing you, and you kept us at arm's length. Then you went back to work and something terrible happened." She squeezed his fingers. "You're not to blame, son. But the only way you're ever going to believe that is if you talk about it and share it and forgive yourself. And to do that, you need to let someone in."

Someone. *Lauren.*

"I can't," he said quietly. "I can't do that to her. Not after what she's been through. I can't promise her everything and potentially leave her with nothing. Not like Dad—"

"Nothing?" his mom said, and cut him off. "Do you think your father left me with nothing?" Her eyes glistened. "Gabe, your dad left me *everything.* He left me four incredible children and the memories of a wonderful life. Do you honestly think our marriage was defined by those last few years?"

Did he? Had he been so wrapped up in making sure they still worked as a family that he'd forgotten what it was like before his father became ill?

"I don't, not for one minute," his mother said earnestly, "resent a single moment of the time I spent caring for your dad when he was sick. He was my husband and the father of my children. He was my rock. My center." Tears welled in her eyes. "And I was honored that he trusted me when he was at his most vulnerable and let me care for him right up until the end."

Gabe swallowed the emotion in his throat. He remembered what Lauren had said to him about trust. She'd said Tim hadn't trusted her. She said he didn't trust her, either. And she was right. He didn't trust easily. Because he was afraid. Of being really seen. Of being considered less than strong and whole. Of being weak. And Lauren saw through that. She saw it all and had still wanted him. And like a fool, he'd pushed her away.

He looked at his mother. "You asked me a question a week ago, and I lied to you."

Her eyes widened. "What question?"

"You asked me if I was in love with her."

Claire Vitali smiled. "And are you?"

Gabe took a breath, felt the air fill his lungs and give him strength and nodded. "Yes, I'm completely and hopelessly in love with Lauren Jakowski."

Chapter Fourteen

Lauren was with a client on Monday afternoon and had finished lacing up the back panel on a beautiful beaded lace gown when a deliveryman arrived, carrying an extravagant floral arrangement. Her first thought was that they were from Steve, and although she considered it a bit too much after only two dates, flipped open the card and looked for his name.

Wrong.

No name. Just a message and an initial.

"Can we talk? G."

Not from Steve. He wasn't trying to change her mind about seeing him again. He'd texted her that morning to arrange another date. A text she'd put off replying to because she didn't want to lead him on. Then he'd called, and she'd declined his offer to go out that week. He was nice. But that was all. He'd taken her refusal easily and wished her well for the future.

She looked at the message again. Gabe. And he wanted to talk? As far as she was concerned, she'd said all she intended saying. They were done and dusted. She tossed the note in the trash and told Dawn, the salesclerk, to take the flowers home.

There was a note pinned to her door when she arrived home. "I would really like to talk with you." More talk? She scrunched the note in a ball and tossed it over the hedge and onto his front lawn.

Flowers arrived again the following day. Her mother and Dawn thought it was incredibly romantic. So did Cassie, when she relayed the story to her best friend. Mary-Jayne called her, too. And Grace. But she wasn't going to be swayed. She didn't want to talk to him. He'd had his chance, and he'd blown it.

On Wednesday, the flower deliveryman had a huge smile on his face when he entered the store. Lauren sent the young man away, flowers in hand, and felt an odd burst of triumph that she'd stuck by her guns. Of course, when she arrived home and found Gabe sitting on her porch steps, flanked by Jed, who wore a silly white bandana around his neck while Gabe held up a tiny white flag, her icy reserve thawed for a brief moment. Until she remembered he'd pushed her away time and time again.

"What's this?" she demanded, and flung her bag over her shoulder.

Gabe smiled and patted the dog on the head. "I borrowed him from your brother. I needed an ally."

She raised a brow and looked at the ridiculous flag. "You're looking for a truce?"

"I was thinking more along the lines of a complete surrender."

Her heart pounded. It was a romantic notion. But she wasn't falling for it. "I hear your family's still in town?"

"Yes," he replied, and got to his feet. The dog followed and rushed toward Lauren. "My mother would very much like to meet you properly."

"I can't imagine why." Lauren laughed loudly. "Since I intend to forget all about you, there's no point."

"You'll never forget me," he said, and stepped closer. "I'll bet that you'll remember me for the rest of your life."

Lauren laughed again. Egotistical jerk. "Have you been drinking?"

"I'm perfectly sober. Why did you send my flowers back today?" he asked.

"Because I don't want flowers or anything else from you."

He reached out and touched her hair, twirling the strands through his fingers. "The flowers are just a place to start."

"A place to start what?" she asked suspiciously as she pulled back from his touch.

"Our courtship."

"Courtship?" She laughed at the old-fashioned word and thrust her hands on her hips.

He *was* drunk. There was no other explanation. And he looked as if he was thinking of kissing her. Which was out of the question. She stepped back and frowned. "Why on earth would I want to do that?"

Gabe smiled that killer smile. "How about because you're in love with me?"

She laughed again, because she didn't know what else to do amidst the madness. "You're out of your mind. I'm going inside. Don't even think of following me."

"You didn't deny it."

"Because…because it's too ridiculous, and because I'm tired of this conversation."

She raced up the steps and fiddled with the door lock. She looked around, hoping he was gone. But no such luck. He stood at the bottom of the steps. Her body shook thinking about how handsome he looked, even holding the silly flag.

"I'll be here tomorrow," he said quietly. "Just in case you change your mind."

She frowned. "Don't you have to work?"

"I quit," he said softly. "I'm going back to medicine. I start in the E.R. at Bellandale Hospital next month."

"Good for you," she said extra sweetly.

"Don't you want to know why?"

She shrugged. "It's not my business."

He stared at her and didn't bother hiding the wounded expression. But she had no intention of backing down. He didn't have the right to simply snap his fingers and expect her to come running.

"I want to be the best man I can be…for you."

"What's the point?" she said flatly.

"Because I…I…"

"Good night, Gabe," she said exasperatedly. She unlocked the door. "And incidentally, I think courtship is meant to start before two people sleep together. We've had this back to front from the very beginning, and that's all the sign I need. And stop sending me flowers. I don't want them or anything else from you." Then she headed inside without looking back.

"Have you tried talking to her again?"

Romantic advice seemed to come out of the woodwork, Gabe discovered, when it became obvious to everyone he knew that Lauren wasn't about to forgive him anytime soon. This time it was his mother, who'd decided to hang around in Crystal Point for another week and dispense counsel about his failures to get Lauren's attention at every opportunity.

"Maybe it's time I had a talk with her," she suggested, and pushed her tea aside.

"You need another approach," a voice said from the doorway.

It was Cameron. *Great.* He was in for the big-brother talk. "Your point?"

Gabe figured he'd tried every approach he knew. He'd been on her doorstep each afternoon for the past four days, and she'd simply ignored him and gone into her house and locked the door. There were calls she wouldn't return, notes she wouldn't read and flowers she sent back. And he had a diamond ring in his pocket he wanted to give her, but was convinced she'd toss it in the trash. Total emasculation wasn't in his plans.

He'd wait. And hope she'd come around.

"No risk, no prize."

Cameron again. And this time, Scott and Aaron were behind him. Gabe looked up and scowled. "What?"

"Is she worth it?"

It was a stupid question, and with his patience frayed, Gabe dismissed the question with a barely audible grunt.

"Is she worth risking everything for?" Cameron asked again, relentless.

Gabe straightened in his seat. "Yes."

"Then tell her that."

In that moment, Gabe realized that he'd been so busy trying to woo Lauren with flowers and dinner invitations, he'd neglected to do the one thing he should have done an age ago.

Tell her the truth. Risking everything meant telling her everything. Like she'd told him time and time again. She'd trusted him. First with her past, then her body and then her heart. It was time he did the same. Because she knew what he'd been through and hadn't turned away. She accepted and wanted him. No questions. No prejudice. *No fear.* When, because of what she'd been through with Tim, she'd had every reason to run and not look back. But she hadn't. She'd put her heart on the line and he'd smashed it. Instead of applauding her courage and embracing that love, he'd brought up a whole load of excuses and reasons why they couldn't be together.

And one reason in particular.

Because he was scared of dying. Scared of living.

He let out a deep breath and looked at her brother. "So what's your big suggestion?"

Cameron grinned. "Well, asking her to forgive you for being a stupid ass hasn't worked, has it?"

Gabe thought about the flowers and the notes and the restrained effort he'd shown during the week. He talked about caring and wanting, and laughed at her attempts to ignore him. But he hadn't told her what she wanted to hear. "Not so far."

"Well, I reckon it's time for you to start begging and prove to her you'll do anything you have to do to win her heart."

And that, Gabe thought with a weary laugh, might just work.

Lauren was ever thankful that Saturday mornings were always busy at the store. It kept her mind away from thinking about anything else. Or anyone else. Or someone in particular.

A bridal party arrived at ten for their final fittings, and when the bride emerged from the changing room in her dress, Lauren set to work, fluffing the three layers of tulle and organza before she adjusted the straps and stepped away so the client's mother and attendants could admire her. When the fitting was complete and the bride was out of her gown, Lauren handed the client over to Dawn to process the sale and bag up the goods.

The bell above the door dinged and Lauren smiled when Cassie and Mary-Jayne entered the store.

"Hi, there," she said, and looked at her friends. "What are you both doing here?"

Cassie grinned. "Reinforcements."

"Huh?"

Her friend shrugged and kept smiling. "Trust me."

"You know I—" The door opened again. The bell dinged. And Gabe's mother walked into her store.

"Good morning, Lauren," she said before Lauren had a chance to move. "I'm not sure if you remember me from last week—I'm Claire Vitali." She grabbed her hand and squeezed it gently.

Lauren stared at the older woman. She had the same eyes as her son, the same smile. There was kindness in her expression and warmth in her hand. Her resolve to stay strong wavered. But she wasn't about to be easily swayed.

"It's nice to meet you," she said, and withdrew her hand. "I'd like to stay and talk but I have to—"

"It can wait," Mary-Jayne said with one of her famous grins.

The door opened again, and Grace and Evie entered.

Lauren frowned. "What's going on?"

"Reinforcements, like I said," Cassie explained.

Panic rushed through her blood. Something was wrong. "Has something happened? Is it my dad, or Cameron or—"

"You're father is fine," her mother said as she emerged from the stockroom.

"So is your brother," Grace added.

Lauren backed up. "I don't think—"

"That's just it, Lauren," Cassie said gently. "Stop thinking. At least, stop *overthinking*. We're all here because we care about you."

She stilled as realization dawned. "So this is, what, an intervention? That's why you're all here?"

"Actually, I think they're all here to stand point and make sure I do the right thing."

Gabe...

She hadn't heard him come through the door. He moved around Evie and Grace and stood near the counter. Lauren remained rooted where she was. Her legs turned to Jell-O. Her heart raced like a freight train. She looked at her family and friends. They were smiling, all hopeful, all clearly wondering what she would do next.

I wish I knew.

It was hard not to stare at Gabe. He looked so good, and she'd missed him. But he'd hurt her. And she didn't want to be hurt again.

"This isn't the right time or place to have this discussion," she said, and tried to politely ignore the bridal party hovering behind her.

"Since you won't talk to me, I reckon it's the only time," he said, and flashed her customers a breathtaking smile. "I'm sure everyone will understand."

The bride nodded, and before Lauren had a chance to protest, her mother had subtly ushered the bridal party from the store.

"What do you want?" she asked as stiffly as she could once the customers were gone.

He took a breath. "First, to apologize."

Lauren shuttled her gaze to her mother, Claire Vitali, Cassie and the other women and saw they were all smiling. Like they knew exactly what was going on. "Okay— apology accepted. You can *all* go now."

But they didn't move.

"I mean it," she said crossly. "Don't think just because you'd managed to swindle everyone into coming here today that I'm going to simply forget everything you've said and done and—"

"They volunteered," he said.

She looked at the sea of faces. "I don't believe it."

"You should. They care about you and only want to see you happy."

"Exactly," she said, and frowned. "Which has nothing to do with you."

"It has everything to do with me," he shot back. "I make you happy."

"You make me mad," she snapped.

"Well, I'd make you happy if you'd let me."

She forced her hands to her hips. "And how do you propose to do that?"

"I'll get to the proposing in a moment. Now, where were we? Oh, yes, I was—"

"What?" Her eyes bulged. "You're going to propose?"

"Well, of course I'm going to propose. But back to what I was saying. Oh, yes…and second," he said, and came a little closer, "I'd like to tell you a story."

"A story?" she echoed vaguely, certain she'd just imagined that he said he was about to propose. "I don't know what—"

"It's a story about a man who thought he was invincible." He spoke so softly she almost strained to hear, but she was quickly mesmerized by the seductive tone of his voice. "He thought nothing and no one could touch him. He went to medical school and became a doctor and spent his days trying to fix people who were broken. But underneath that facade of caring and compassion, he was arrogant and stubborn and always did what he wanted because he thought he knew best. And then one day he was told he was sick and everything changed. He wasn't strong. He wasn't healthy. Now he was broken but he couldn't fix himself. He had the surgery and the treatment, but because he was stubborn and arrogant, he went back to work before he should have."

Lauren's throat closed over. Her heart was breaking for him. His pain was palpable, and she longed to fall into his arms. She had been so attuned to him, she hadn't noticed that their mothers and friends had somehow left the store. Everyone was outside and they were alone. She could see them through the big front window. They were smiling. And suddenly, she almost felt like smiling, too. Right now, in front of her, lay her future. But she didn't smile. Because he was opening up, and she wanted to hear everything.

"Gabe, I—"

"I went back to work too early," he said, his voice thick. "I didn't listen. I didn't want to hear it. I just wanted to prove that I was the same. That I wasn't damaged and somehow less than the man I once was. Less than the doctor I once was. But while I was in the bathroom throwing up from the side effects of the medication I was on, the woman and her baby came into the E.R. I wasn't there. And she died, along with her baby. All because I wouldn't admit that I *was* changed. That I was suddenly not just a man. Not just a doctor. I was a cancer patient. And it felt as though those words defined me, made me, *owned* me."

Her entire body shuddered. The raw honesty in his words melted her. "That's why you quit being a doctor? Because you believed that patient died because you were sick? Because you were somehow less than who you used to be?"

"Yes."

Her expression softened. "But you're not."

"I know that now," he said, and smiled. "I know that because when you look at me, I know you don't see a patient. You don't see a man who was sick. You just see…me."

He stepped closer, and Lauren swayed toward him. "Of course I do."

"Doesn't anything scare you, Lauren?" he asked, and took her hand. "After what you went through with Tim, doesn't the very idea of being with me make you want to run?"

"I've only ever seen you, Gabe. Not the doctor, not the patient. The man…the man who has listened to me and comforted me and makes me feel more alive than anyone else ever has. A man who's kind and considerate and has never judged me. And I'm not scared."

He pulled her gently toward him.

"The only thing I'm scared of is waking up and finding that this is a dream."

"It's no dream," he said softly. "You must know that I'm in love with you."

Did Gabe just say he loved me?

She shook her head, not quite prepared to believe him. "No, you're not."

"I am," he said, and touched her cheek. "I love you. I love

that you make me laugh. I love that you tell me when I'm being an egotistical jerk. And I love that you had the courage to let me into your heart when you had every reason not to."

Lauren blinked back tears. "But…you said you had a plan and wouldn't—"

"A stupid plan," he said, and grasped her hand. "I was wrapped up in self-pity and afraid to get involved, and you knew it. You saw through me, Lauren, and still…still wanted me. Even when you knew there was a chance it might not be forever, or I could get sick again. Or I might not be able to give you the children you want." He linked their fingers. "You talk straight and make the complicated simple. You told me how you felt and it spooked me. I'm not proud of my behavior these past weeks, and I promise I'll always be honest about my feelings with you from this day. You have such incredible strength…a strength you don't even know you possess."

Lauren swayed, felt his arms beckoning her. He looked solemn, sincere and wholly lovable. "I don't know…I'm not sure I can."

He squeezed her fingers. "You can, Lauren. Trust me…I won't hurt you again."

"Trust you?" She looked at the sea of faces peering through the windows. "Even though you dragged my friends and family here today to give you an advantage?"

He smiled. "It was Cameron's idea. He thought if I made a big enough fool out of myself in front of our families, you just might just show mercy and forgive me for being an idiot." He came closer until they were almost touching. "I love you, Lauren. I think I've loved you from the moment I pulled you from that swimming pool. And I'm sorry I haven't said it sooner."

He really loves me? Her legs wobbled, and he took her in his arms. "You're not going to completely ruin my reputation and kiss me in front of all these people who are staring at us through the window, are you?"

"I certainly am."

She heard whoops and sighs from the people outside, and Lauren laughed. It felt good. She thawed a little more. Gabe's love was what she wanted. *All* she wanted. And suddenly having the whole world know it didn't bother Lauren in the slightest. He was right—she was strong. Strong enough to open her heart again. And strong enough to cope with whatever the future brought them. He'd pushed past his fears to claim her, and she loved him all the more for it.

"But first," he said, and stepped back a little, "I have to ask you a question."

"What question is that?" she teased, and grinned foolishly.

Gabe dropped to one knee in front of her. "Marry me?" he asked, and pulled a small box from his pocket. The lid flipped open and she saw the perfectly cut diamond, which glittered like his eyes. "When you're ready, when you trust me enough, marry me, Lauren?"

Lauren touched his face and held out her left hand and sighed. "I think you've made a big enough fool out of yourself today for me to know I can trust you, Gabe. And my answer is yes. I'll marry you. I love you." She grinned. "And I kind of like the idea of being a doctor's wife."

Gabe got to his feet, slipped the ring onto her finger and kissed her. "I have you to thank for making me see sense, for making me realize how much I've missed my work. I was afraid to go back. I was afraid to try to recapture what I'd lost. But knowing you and loving you has made me stronger. You make me whole."

Lauren returned his kiss with every ounce of love in her heart. "You're the love of my life, Gabe."

His gaze narrowed. "I thought—"

"You," she said, and touched his face. "Only you. I did love Tim, but honestly, anything I've felt in the past feels a bit like kid stuff compared to the way I love you. And want you. And need you."

His eyes glistened. "Thank you. And while I may not be the first man you've loved, I'm honored to be the one you love now."

"Now and forever." She pressed against him and smiled. "But, Gabe, where are we going to live? Your place or mine?"

"How about neither?" he suggested. "How about we find somewhere new? A new home for a new beginning."

"I like the sound of that," Lauren said, and accepted his kiss. "And I'd like to get a dog," she said breathlessly when the kissing stopped.

He grinned. "Anything you want."

Lauren curved against him. "And babies?"

His arms tightened around her, and he smiled. "I'll see what I can do."

She sighed. "I'm not worried, Gabe. I want to marry you and have your baby. But if there's only ever us, that will be enough."

"You're sure?"

"Never surer."

She kissed him again, knowing she finally had her happy ending.

* * * * *

Don't miss Cassie's story,
Coming in early 2015!
Available wherever Harlequin books are sold.

COMING NEXT MONTH FROM

HARLEQUIN®

SPECIAL EDITION

Available September 23, 2014

#2359 TEXAS BORN • by Diana Palmer

Michelle Godfrey might be young, but she's fallen hard for Gabriel Brandon, the rugged rancher who rescued her from a broken home. Over time, their bond grows, and Gabriel eventually realizes there's more to his affection than just a protective instinct. But Michelle stumbles on Gabriel's deepest secrets, putting their lives—and their love—in jeopardy.

#2360 THE EARL'S PREGNANT BRIDE

The Bravo Royales • by Christine Rimmer

Genevra Bravo-Calabretti might be a princess of Montedoro, but that doesn't mean she doesn't make mistakes. When one night with the devilishly handsome Rafael DeValery, Earl of Hartmore, results in a surprise pregnancy, Genny can't believe it. Meanwhile, Rafe is determined to make her his bride. Will the fairy-tale couple get a happily-ever-after of their very own?

#2361 THE LAST-CHANCE MAVERICK

Montana Mavericks: 20 Years in the Saddle! • by Christyne Butler

Vanessa Brent might be a famous artist, but not even she can paint a happy ending for her best friend. Following her late BFF's instructions, Vanessa moves to Rust Creek Falls to find true happiness, which is where she meets architect Jonah Dalton. He's looking to rebuild his own life after a painful divorce, but little does each know that the other might be the key to true love.

#2362 DIAMOND IN THE RUFF

Matchmaking Mamas • by Marie Ferrarella

Pastry chef Lily Langtry can whip up delicious desserts with ease...but finding a boyfriend? That's a bit harder. The Matchmaking Mamas decide to take matters into their own hands and gift Lily with an adorable puppy that needs some extra TLC—from handsome veterinarian Dr. Christopher Whitman! Can the canine bring together Lily and Christopher in a *paws*-itively perfect romance?

#2363 THE RANCHER WHO TOOK HER IN

The Bachelors of Blackwater Lake • by Teresa Southwick

Kate Scott is a bride on the lam when she shows up at Cabot Dixon's Montana ranch. Her commitment-shy host is still reeling from his wife's abandonment of their family. But Cabot's son, Tyler, decides that Kate is going to be his new mom, and his dad can't help but be intrigued by Blackwater Lake's latest addition. Will Kate and Cabot each get a second chance at a happy ending?

#2364 ONE NIGHT WITH THE BEST MAN • by Amanda Berry

Ever since the end of her relationship with Dr. Luke Ward, Penny Montgomery has said "no" to long-term love. But seeing Luke again changes everything. He's the best man at his brother's wedding, and maid of honor Penny is determined to rekindle the sparks with her former flame, but just temporarily. However, love doesn't always follow the rules.... _____

HSECNM0914

REQUEST YOUR FREE BOOKS!
2 FREE NOVELS PLUS 2 FREE GIFTS!

⊕ HARLEQUIN®

SPECIAL EDITION

Life, Love & Family

YES! Please send me 2 FREE Harlequin® Special Edition novels and my 2 FREE gifts (gifts are worth about $10). After receiving them, if I don't wish to receive any more books, I can return the shipping statement marked "cancel." If I don't cancel, I will receive 6 brand-new novels every month and be billed just $4.74 per book in the U.S. or $5.24 per book in Canada. That's a savings of at least 14% off the cover price! It's quite a bargain! Shipping and handling is just 50¢ per book in the U.S. and 75¢ per book in Canada.* I understand that accepting the 2 free books and gifts places me under no obligation to buy anything. I can always return a shipment and cancel at any time. Even if I never buy another book, the two free books and gifts are mine to keep forever.

235/335 HDN F45Y

Name _____ (PLEASE PRINT)

Address _____ Apt. #

City _____ State/Prov. _____ Zip/Postal Code

Signature (if under 18, a parent or guardian must sign)

Mail to the Harlequin® Reader Service:
IN U.S.A.: P.O. Box 1867, Buffalo, NY 14240-1867
IN CANADA: P.O. Box 609, Fort Erie, Ontario L2A 5X3

Want to try two free books from another line?
Call 1-800-873-8635 or visit www.ReaderService.com.

* Terms and prices subject to change without notice. Prices do not include applicable taxes. Sales tax applicable in N.Y. Canadian residents will be charged applicable taxes. Offer not valid in Quebec. This offer is limited to one order per household. Not valid for current subscribers to Harlequin Special Edition books. All orders subject to credit approval. Credit or debit balances in a customer's account(s) may be offset by any other outstanding balance owed by or to the customer. Please allow 4 to 6 weeks for delivery. Offer available while quantities last.

Your Privacy—The Harlequin® Reader Service is committed to protecting your privacy. Our Privacy Policy is available online at www.ReaderService.com or upon request from the Harlequin Reader Service.

We make a portion of our mailing list available to reputable third parties that offer products we believe may interest you. If you prefer that we not exchange your name with third parties, or if you wish to clarify or modify your communication preferences, please visit us at www.ReaderService.com/consumerschoice or write to us at Harlequin Reader Service Preference Service, P.O. Box 9062, Buffalo, NY 14269. Include your complete name and address.

HSE13R

***

Just for an instant, Gabriel worried about putting Michelle
in the line of fire, considering his line of work. He had
enemies. Dangerous enemies who wouldn't hesitate to
threaten anyone close to him. Of course, there was his
sister, Sara, but she'd lived in Wyoming for the past few
years, away from him, on a ranch they co-owned. Now he
was putting her in jeopardy along with Michelle.

But what could he do? The child had nobody. Now that
her idiot stepmother, Roberta, was dead, Michelle was truly
on her own. It was dangerous for a young woman to live
alone, even in a small community. And there was also the
question of Roberta's boyfriend, Bert.

Gabriel knew things about the man that he wasn't eager to share with Michelle. Bert was part of a criminal organization, and he knew Michelle's habits. He also had a yen for her, if what Michelle had blurted out to Gabriel once was true—and he had no indication that she would lie about it. Bert might decide to come try his luck with her now that her stepmother was out of the picture. That couldn't be allowed.

Gabriel was surprised by his own affection for Michelle. It wasn't paternal. She was, of course, far too young for anything heavy. She was a beauty, kind and generous and sweet. She was the sort of woman he usually ran from. No, strike that, she was no woman. She was still unfledged, a dove without flight feathers. He had to keep his interest hidden. At least, until she was grown up enough that it wouldn't hurt his conscience to pursue her. Afterward…well, who knew the future?

***

Don't miss TEXAS BORN
by New York Times *bestselling author Diana Palmer,*
the latest installment in
THE LONG, TALL TEXANS *miniseries.*

Available October 2014 wherever
Harlequin® Special Edition books and ebooks are sold.

HARLEQUIN®

SPECIAL EDITION

Life, Love and Family

Coming in October 2014

THE EARL'S PREGNANT BRIDE

by *NEW YORK TIMES* bestselling author

Christine Rimmer

Genevra Bravo-Calabretti might be a princess of Montedoro, but that doesn't mean she's doesn't make mistakes. When one night with the devilishly handsome Rafael DeValery, Earl of Hartmore, results in a surprise pregnancy, Genny can't believe it. Meanwhile, Rafe is determined to make her his bride. Will the fairy-tale couple get a happily-ever-after of their very own?

Don't miss the latest edition of
THE BRAVO ROYALES *continuity!*

Available wherever books and ebooks are sold!

HSE65842

SPECIAL EDITION

Life, Love and Family

THE LAST-CHANCE MAVERICK
The latest edition of
MONTANA MAVERICKS: 20 YEARS IN THE SADDLE!
by *USA TODAY* bestselling author

Christyne Butler

Vanessa Brent might be a famous artist, but not even she can paint a happy ending for her best friend. Following her late BFF's instructions, Vanessa moves to Rust Creek Falls to find true happiness, which is where she meets architect Jonah Dalton. He's looking to rebuild his own life after a painful divorce, but little does each know that the other might be the key to true love.

Available October 2014
wherever books and ebooks are sold!

Catch up on the first three stories in
MONTANA MAVERICKS: 20 YEARS IN THE SADDLE!

MILLION-DOLLAR MAVERICK
by Christine Rimmer

FROM MAVERICK TO DADDY
by Teresa Southwick

MAVERICK FOR HIRE
by Leanne Banks

www.Harlequin.com